G000096602

THE MISSING
MONSIEUR
MAX

By the same author:

All Through the Night
Keeping the Lid On
and
Spy Without a Cause

The Missing
Monsieur Max

Neil Thomas

THOROGOOD

Published by Thorogood
10-12 Rivington Street
London EC2A 3DU

Telephone: 020 7749 4748
Email: info@thorogoodpublishing.co.uk
Web: www.thorogoodpublishing.co.uk

A CIP catalogue record for this book is available
from the British Library.

ISBN paperback: 9781854189141
ISBN eBook: 9781854189158

Designed by: Driftdesign Ltd
www.getyourdrift.com

For Cheryl – my partner in crime – and Ella,
and all our happy times in France

1.

St Rémy de Provence's answer to Inspector Maigret was sitting outside the Bistrot des Alpilles, shaded from the unforgiving sun by the awning the patron had just extended over the terrace.

Commandant Ruppert, with his empty notebook open in front of him, was wondering how the great detective himself might have approached a case like this.

An expat Englishman, Clive Collins, was missing.

After a report by the man's caretaker, uniform had visited the house, turning up his passport and car keys. Three weeks of the usual checks by the missing persons section of the Gendarmerie Nationale had drawn a blank.

Ruppert, based in Avignon, living in St Rémy, had been called in by the examining magistrate and asked to take over the investigation of the mysterious disappearance. He was told that the British Consulate in Marseilles had kicked up a right old fuss about it and the English relatives were causing a stink in the British media.

He'd read the file. No hard evidence or clues. No worthwhile leads established . . . what *had* they been doing? He knew he'd have to follow up with the people already contacted, but he needed something new.

He held a photo of the missing man out in front of him. The patron, bringing him his usual café noisette, saw it and couldn't resist commenting.

'Ah, that's Monsieur Max. Are you working on his case, Commandant? We all hope nothing sinister has happened.'

'Monsieur Max?'

'That's how we know him. Something about living life to the max, I think. Everyone calls him that.'

Looking at the picture carefully, Ruppert saw a man not bad for seventy who clearly knew how to widen his eyes, smile and tilt his head for the camera. You couldn't read the face, as the expression was strangely false. The eyes were alert, but not kindly. The expression and the mouth itself, whilst not exactly cruel, were slightly unpleasant. He cared about his appearance, that was obvious, but the beige linen suit and checked shirt gave him a dated look – one, if anything, older than his face.

Across the road from where he was paying for his morning coffee were the offices of the estate agency most likely to have sold Clive Collins a house in the town. He'd pay them a visit some time. His friend Philippe ran it and, like all estate agents, could be relied on to know more about them than his clients ever could imagine.

He put his notebook in his jacket pocket. He knew what he had to do next.

*   *   *

Ruppert was soon walking along the tree-shaded boulevards that circle the small centre of St Rémy to meet up with Gérard Paquet, who kept an eye on Clive Collins' house when he was away and acted as its guardian.

Linking up, as arranged, at the church of St Martin, they introduced themselves on its wide entrance steps and set off for the nearby house, talking as they walked.

'When did you last see the Monsieur?'

'About three weeks ago.'

'And you've heard nothing since?'

'No and, in the normal course of events, that isn't strange. He only contacts me if he's going away.'

'How often is that?'

'From time to time he goes back to London to see family and gets me to drive him to Nîmes to catch a flight, or to Avignon to get the train.'

'Does he travel elsewhere?'

'Not really. Maybe short trips to the Riviera, sometimes

into the Camargue, or to see friends in the area, but then he wouldn't need to tell me. Only if he's likely to be away for more than a few days am I needed to look in on the house.'

'Why did you report him missing?'

'His son rang me to say he couldn't contact him and asked me to check the house. There was no sign of him there. Using a list of numbers by the phone, I made a few calls to the names I recognised as his main friends and none of them had heard from him. I reported back to the family and it was agreed that I should phone the gendarmerie.'

'Has he ever gone anywhere before without telling you? Is it totally out of character?'

'His disappearance is odd . . . worrying. It's not like him at all. He's usually precise about everything . . . too fussy, if anything, always making sure I know the exact dates of where he'll be and when.'

'What do you think has happened to him?'

'I've no idea. At first I thought he might be with a friend, but as the days passed I got increasingly concerned. It's not like him. He would've been in touch as he's always worried about the house when he's away from it.'

'How long have you known him?'

'About ten years, from when he first bought the place. My wife worked at the estate agency handling the sale and, when asked to recommend someone who could speak English to mind it for him, she suggested me as I was between jobs and could do things in the garden or the house.'

'So you know him well?'

'Hardly. Since he started living here, pretty much full time about five years ago, I go to the house less often, mainly when he isn't there.'

'You must have formed an impression of him?'

'Ah. This is the house.' Gérard had ignored the question as he fumbled for the keys. A bit guarded even for a guardian, thought Ruppert.

You couldn't tell from the road what lay behind the high wall and grey panelled metal gates. Inside, a small black Citroën C3 was positioned under a chestnut tree. The house was a low two-storey property with an attractive terrace and small fenced-in pool to the side of it. White wisteria blooms hung from an overhead trellis covering a large outside dining table and chairs. Around the perimeter, by the wall, were tall thin cypresses, an impressive olive tree and large oleander bushes. Ruppert strolled about, admiringly, looking up at the other houses and wondering what the neighbours could tell him.

Whilst he did that, Gérard was unlocking the double doors into the house and, as he pushed them open, Ruppert followed him in.

'Is it strange the car is here?'

'Not really. He rarely uses it.'

They were straight into the kitchen of the house where everything seemed in order. It was a mix of old and new with typical artefacts that only foreigners thought the French would have.

'I can make you a black coffee whilst you look around, if you like.'

'Thanks ... where do you suggest I start?'

'Through that door there,' he said, pointing to a room off the kitchen. 'That's his study.'

*   *   *

There were plenty of books and CDs on sturdy shelving and Ruppert, bending his neck sideways to read, scanned the titles, which were in English and didn't mean much to him.

The desk was unusually large for a relatively small space and it was covered with green folders in neat piles, surprisingly tidy given that uniform had been in. Sitting in the desk chair, he swivelled it to one side of the desk where there was a filing cabinet that had been forced open. That's more like it, he thought. He shouted through to the kitchen, 'Gérard, what happened to these drawers?'

'I didn't have the key. They had to force it, but I don't know what they found. I never knew what was in there.'

Opening it, and wondering whether Gérard had

been through it since, Ruppert found very methodically arranged files. He could see that Monsieur Max kept his paperwork in order. That might prove helpful.

Coffee was brought in and Gérard took the offered seat opposite.

'What did the officers remove from the house?'

'Only his address book, his calendar, the passport and the car keys. Nothing else. They stayed most of the morning and went through the papers here in the house and I answered any queries as best I could. They told me not to touch anything or it would be bad for me.'

'I'll come back this afternoon and go through everything again. Can you be here at two thirty?'

'Certainly, it's my day off as it happens.'

'What do you do?'

'I work at St Paul de Mausole.'

'At the psychiatric hospital there?'

'No, Monsieur, the Van Gogh museum.'

'Oh, I see. Then I'm sorry to intrude on your day off.'

'That's all right. I want to help and get this all settled.'

'I've a few questions, now, if you don't mind. First of all, does Monsieur Max – if that's how you know him along with everyone else – have any enemies that you know of?'

'Yes, most people call him Monsieur Max.'

'I'll ask you again – any enemies you can think of?'

'He falls out with people all the time, but enemies as such, I'd say no.'

'Who has he fallen out with?'

'I'm not sure. I can't say and, anyway, I can't talk about his private affairs, I'm sorry.'

'What on earth do you mean?'

'He made me sign a non-disclosure contract when I took the job. He said he always did that with employees or domestic staff – so I can't talk about confidential matters, I'm afraid.'

Ruppert was surprised at this statement and couldn't hide it.

'What? You do realise, don't you, that you're possibly the last person to see Monsieur Max and that this could well turn out to be a murder case? I think you'd better forget about the gagging clauses in your contract and think of helping to save your own skin.'

'What do you mean? He's missing, that's all. Why do you think he was murdered? Maybe he's had an accident or a heart attack out in the Alpilles. I've already said that and told the other policemen his favourite spot was out by the Roman reservoir.'

'That search obviously drew a blank and, assuming he never went off piste when walking in the hills, his body would probably have been found by now by other walkers or their dogs.'

'Could he have fallen some way from the track perhaps?'

'Thanks for your theories, but answer the question.'

'Well, Monsieur Max is fond of women, Commandant, and has many female friends. Some are married and maybe their husbands ...'

'Was he ever threatened?'

'Not that he shared with me, but there was one time when the front gates were daubed with graffiti that I had to clean off.'

'What did it say?'

'Adulterer ... in big red letters.'

'What was his reaction?'

'He was very calm about it. He smiled and said, "They must have got the wrong house, Gérard. It can't be me ... I'm not married." '

'What do you think?'

'I think it *was* the right house, but, technically, the wrong word maybe. He wasn't married, that's true, although he'd been married twice before and given it up for good, or so he said.'

'Any ideas who did the graffiti?'

'Other than the husband of one of his married conquests, no.'

'That suggests there could be a long queue?'

'I think so, perhaps.'

'This afternoon, Gérard, you and I are going to have a nice long chat and a look at the address book and calendar, once I've retrieved them. I expect you to be open with me. Understood?'

'Yes, Monsieur.'

*　　　*　　　*

As he strolled back in the intense heat of midday to his home for lunch, stopping on his way to pick up a baguette in Rue Carnot, Ruppert tried to see what he made of things so far. Of Gérard, he was unsure. Intense, yes. Intelligent, yes. Honest? Who knows?

As for Monsieur Max ... well, still clearly a ladies' man, a player, an aged lothario, whatever. The confidentiality stuff implied to Ruppert a certain type of character – in his experience, people who were secretive always had something to hide.

Arriving at his house on Rue Lucien Estrine, opposite the glass blower's shop, he could tell Madame Ruppert had also popped home too, because the first floor window was open and he could hear the radio. Once inside, as he climbed the stone steps to the first floor, she called out to him.

'You're home then. Not much on?'

Walking in and giving her an affectionate peck on the cheek, he explained, 'I've been saddled with a missing persons case – but it could prove to be a challenging one.'

'More mealtimes with you staring into the middle distance then, I suppose,' she said, switching off the news bulletin.

He was pleased to see her and, happily leaving the

making of the lunch to her, sat sipping the glass of rosé she thoughtfully poured for him.

'It's an Englishman.'

'The one that was on the front of *La Provence* – the old guy who's completely disappeared?'

'That's the one. Clive Collins. Have you seen him before?'

'Of course. Before he went missing, he was always around the town in the cafés and restaurants. Every market day he'd be sitting having lunch at the Créperie Lou Planet in Place Favier. You must have seen him.'

'I don't think so.'

'Really, Jules. Some detective you are. You should try looking *at* people, even when you're not looking *for* them, you know.'

Over the meal of salade niçoise and bread that she had rustled up in no time at all, he asked his wife, 'Tell me then, what did *you* make of Monsieur Collins, if you're such a good detective?'

'I noticed he was either with, or meeting, someone – usually female. I must say he seemed frightfully popular, not at all the sort of man you'd think would just disappear . . . he seemed to be having such a good time.'

'Did you ever recognise any of the women he was with?'

'Not really, no. I did see him once, sitting outside Café Riche with the owner of that gallery on Boulevard Marceau. When she caught my eye as I walked past, she suddenly asked in a loud voice – purely for my benefit,

I'm sure – "What sort of art work *are* you looking for exactly, Monsieur?" '

After coffee and clearing away, Ruppert put on his jacket to leave as his wife asked, 'What time will you be back this evening? Is it going to be a late one? Will you be eating supper with me?'

'Something cold will do. I need to break the back of this case or the magistrate will be breathing down my neck. They're looking for a quick result. Don't wait for me.'

2.

Having picked up the relevant papers at the gendarmerie, Ruppert was back chez Monsieur Max by two thirty,
driven by Lieutenant Bonnet, a bright and breezy young
officer seconded to do some legwork for him on the case.

Gérard was there – the gates and the house were open
– and in they went. Introducing Bonnet, Ruppert asked
if they could have some coffee.

'We'll set up on the kitchen table, so we can work
together when required and spread out. We'll call you if
we need you.'

With Gérard out of the way, busy in the garden,
Ruppert showed Bonnet the study and shared some of
the background from the police notes before setting him
to work going through the bank statements to flag up
anything unusual.

Ruppert found a file on the purchase of the house
and was flicking through it when he was struck by the

fact that the previous owner was Sam Rodgers, a name he recognised at once as the author of a book he'd seen that morning on a shelf in the study.

He took the book down and regretted his lack of English. Maybe his wife would take a look. She'd studied English at university and liked to keep her hand in even now, enjoying reading Georges Simenon books in the English translation, because she found the language simple and straightforward. He could tell this one was a crime book as the blood-stained knife on the cover was a clue even he could understand, and the title, *Assassin,* made it clear enough. He put it to one side – with his case notes – so he'd remember to take the book home with him later.

As he read further about the purchase of the house, sure enough, the estate agent who had handled the sale was his friend, so he called him up there and then. Philippe was guarded on the phone, which was unusual. Maybe he was in a meeting, thought Ruppert, and he hurried the call, diplomatically arranging to see him later for a drink at six, at the Café des Arts.

'What have *you* found, Bonnet? Anything useful?'

'Nothing yet. There was a lot of money spent on work by Taval the plumber last year, maybe for the pool judging by the amounts involved. He was obviously paying by cheque. You don't see that often – an honest man for a change.'

'More likely he either wanted proof of payment, if

anything went wrong and there was a dispute, or perhaps he needed to keep a record for capital gains tax purposes.'

'That's very cynical, sir.'

'That's our job, Lieutenant, but you've raised something there. I want you to dig out any papers on house improvements. I think I saw a file on it. See if there *are* any disputes.'

Ruppert walked around the kitchen. By the phone there were a stack of cards, mostly restaurants in the area, but one for Club Paradis Plage in the Camargue stood out and, top of the pile, was a well-used one for TAXI Franck Rachet.

He stuck his head out of the front door and saw Gérard doing some pruning.

'What can you tell me about Franck Rachet?'

'Monsieur Max's preferred taxi driver. He pretty much takes him everywhere.'

'He doesn't seem to have been spoken to by our people. I'll get onto him.'

'I rang him, Monsieur, and he said he hadn't had any contact for a week or so. I told your colleagues that, which might explain why they didn't feel the need to talk to him.'

'Would you mind stepping inside and going through some of these names with me?'

With a sigh, Gérard walked over as Ruppert turned to go back into the kitchen, and, following him in, joined him at the table.

'First of all,' Ruppert said, 'some of the notes I have

on the individuals contacted don't give me any idea of which of them is important in your boss's life. Help me out here ... take these names on the calendar. There are little stars by some of them, look,' he said, pointing to a few at random. 'What do they mean?'

'Can't say.'

'Can't, or won't say?'

'I don't know. Your guess is as good as mine.'

'They appear throughout the calendar, usually by female names. Our boys' notes on file seem only to clarify when those asked had last seen Monsieur Max, not what their relationship was. You'll have to enlighten me, Gérard.'

'I'm really not comfortable doing this, Commandant. Is it really necessary?'

'I'm afraid I must insist.'

'Honestly? All the ones with stars are rather more than just friends and that's not a guess. I think it's a rather unpleasant shorthand note referring to intimate liaisons.'

'Thank you. That confirms my thoughts. I'll start with those, some of whom haven't been approached yet. Do you have the calendar for last year and the year before?'

'Yes, they're in a file on the desk in the study.'

Bonnet, who'd heard this exchange, brought it through, looking at the open file as he did so.

'Here they are, Chief. And, blimey, there are a lot of stars.'

Ruppert smiled, but he was more perturbed by just

how detailed Gérard's knowledge was of his employer's filing system. Maybe confidentiality clauses weren't so weird. He glanced through the previous year's calendar.

'There are a lot of entries with stars for the initials MB followed by "Eygalières". Who is MB and why Eygalières?'

'I really don't know. I know that Monsieur Max was interested in buying an investment property there.'

'I guess he was looking to get his hands on somebody's assets,' quipped Bonnet on his way back to the study – a remark that attracted sideways glances from the other two.

Ruppert went to stand behind Gérard and, stabbing with his finger, went through certain names on the list, asking what their relationship was to Monsieur Max.

'*She* owns a gallery in St Rémy and was a regular visitor here for a while . . . *She's* an English actress who lives over near Les Baux who Monsieur Max visits when her husband is away . . . *She* runs Le Saigon – he dines there some Saturdays and stays over from time to time, I think . . . and *this* one came out here last summer and stayed on after her husband left, although I was told she spent most of the time crying.'

'Good, write down their names and any phone numbers. If you don't mind me saying, you seem to know a lot, considering you're hardly here when your boss is in residence.'

'Monsieur Max tells me what he's up to. I don't want to know, but he's forever commenting on people, running them down one minute or waxing lyrical about them the next. One day he'll be singing their praises and the following day destroying them. I can barely keep up and I never know what he really thinks about anyone. I wonder what he says about *me* behind my back.'

Bonnet drifted in again with the address book. He obviously had big ears, because he asked, 'Do you think the initials MB can be Melanie Beauvais? There are two addresses for her, both in Eygalières, one of them being an estate agency, Agence Maison Lux on Rue de la République, and the other, presumably, her house.'

'Nice work, Bonnet. Ring and find out if she's in her office tomorrow morning for a chat, don't say what about. Oh, and before you do that, ring this taxi guy, Franck what's-his-name. He may be around in town. If he is, get him to call round straight away.'

'By the way, sir' Bonnet added, 'your hunch was right, he was in a big dispute last year with the plumber over problems with the pool, including a leak, and he withheld the final payment of twenty-five thousand euros. We'll have to have a word with the plumber about what happened.'

'Nice work, Bonnet . . . Gérard, what can you tell us about these pool problems?'

'It was unpleasant. There were strong words spoken, I understand, but Monsieur Max didn't seem to be worried – even when I told him to be careful about antagonising a big firm like that. Monsieur Taval has a bit of a reputation, shall we say, about debt collection and there are . . . stories.'

'Like what?'

'A time when he had a contretemps with a German expat who had a large pool installed at his home in Maussane and then refused to pay, saying it wasn't what he was quoted. Neither side would budge. Taval, allegedly, went back when the owner was away in Germany and filled it in with concrete. The police decided that, although the German didn't have his pool, he hadn't paid for one either, so they were at a loss as to what to do. It dragged on until the German later sold the house with "an attractive paved terrace with potential for swimming pool". Taval used to laugh about it, oblivious to the fact it didn't show him in a good light.'

'Was Monsieur Max's dispute with him still going on when he disappeared?'

'Yes, but he'd kept reassuring me, saying a number of times, "It's small beer." The last time I asked him, he said, "Look, Gérard, don't fret. I've told him he'll get his money, in full, when he comes back to fix the leak." '

'Has it been fixed?'

'No, you can still see it . . . at the side of one end of the pool, there's water dripping from the automatic top-up piping.'

Bonnet came back in, at this point. 'By the way, where's the computer? There's a printer, but no computer. Did the missing persons lot take it in?'

Gérard was quick to answer, 'It's gone. I noticed when I first came to check the house to see if he was here. I searched everywhere, but it's not here and it's not in the car.'

'What else did you check for? There's nothing in my notes about a mobile phone.'

'He didn't have one. He said the last thing he wanted was to be bothered by people that he didn't want to speak to. And, I checked for his house keys, wallet and bank cards and found nothing.'

Bonnet couldn't resist saying, 'You should be working for us, Gérard. Your scene of crime work is good. Notice anything else?'

'I listened to the messages on the house phone. Some were in English from his family asking him to call, but most of them were in French, a few sales calls . . . some were from people who had appointments listed on the calendar, so I could tell roughly how long he'd been missing – since around the twelfth of last month. I told all this to the gendarmes who interviewed me.'

Ruppert had the case file open in front of him and, picking up one sheet, said, 'There's a note of those calls here, with helpful translations into French of the English ones, including a fairly long message. It says, "Hi Clive, it's Sam here. I hope to see you next month when I come over for the Festival, you know how much I miss the bull running. Anyway, I'll be staying at the Château des Alpilles this time, so I'll get in touch when I'm there as it would be great to see you again. So long for now . . . Purchaser." Is this the Sam Rodgers who sold him the house?'

'Yes . . . I would think so, but I have to say, from what he told me, Monsieur Max does not count him a friend. He can't avoid seeing him on his return visits to St Rémy, but there's no love lost there, believe me.'

'Where does this Sam Rodgers stay when he isn't at the Château des Alpilles?'

'I think he usually stays at the Hôtel Les Ateliers de l'Image.'

'That's the old Hôtel Provence in the middle of town with the converted cinema extension, isn't it?'

'Yes, that's the one.'

Ruppert consulted the calendar again. 'There's no message from Taval listed, yet, according to this, he was due to come to the house on the fifteenth. That's odd, isn't it, Bonnet . . . unless you know something, Gérard?'

'Taval rang me, Commandant. His angry call about being let down and the anxious ones from the relatives were why I came looking for Monsieur Max in the first place.'

'OK. We'll still see Taval and we'll also pay a visit to Sam Rodgers who must be in town by now as the Festival has already started. Gérard, if you can leave me a spare set of keys to the house, you can feel free to go. We'll lock up. We may need to come back here whilst you're at work over the next few days and having the keys will be useful so we don't have to keep bothering you.'

'Very well, Monsieur. You have my number. Please call me if I can help in any way.'

*   *   *

Whilst Ruppert made some further notes, Bonnet got busy on the phone.

'Good news, sir. Franck Rachet is going to call round here in ten minutes or so, between jobs. Madame Melanie Beauvais, who sounds quite a handful, will see us in the morning, but it must be before midday as she has a "very important client" taking her to lunch.'

'Don't jump to conclusions, Bonnet.'

'Well, I mean, sir, I could practically hear the eyelashes fluttering down the phone.'

'Didn't she ask who you were and why you wanted to see her?'

'By the sound of her, I think she assumes that any male would want to see her, but she did ask for my name and whether I had a property to sell or was looking to buy.'

'What did you say?'

'I told her she came highly recommended and that I wanted to pick her brains about some developing ideas in her area.'

'Subtly done, Bonnet. We'll make a detective of you yet. I like to have an element of surprise when I'm interviewing.'

'I found something else in the bank file, sir. In amongst all the statements from Crédit Agricole there was a printout of a page from a UK bank, National Westminster, which showed thirty thousand euros being issued to Clive Collins round about the time he was buying the house. The fact that he'd filed an English bank item in with the French bank statements looks deliberate. That seems like a lot of cash to me.'

'He might have felt he needed it when he moved in.'

'Yes, but for someone wedded to his chequebook, it seems excessive. And why not draw the cash on his French account? He's certainly got enough in there.'

'Check the date of the cash against the date of completing on the purchase of the house. There might be a link there. It could even be an under-the-table payment – interesting, Bonnet, well done.'

*   *   *

Bursting through the scratching symphony of cicadas, a car came to a crunching halt on the gravel by the front gates, followed by a door slamming and a shout of 'hello'.

'This must be Franck, Bonnet. I'll meet him outside. Bring some glasses of water out and join us. I want you to make some notes.'

They all three sat at the table under the wisteria. Franck was a dark-haired, tanned and lively guy in his forties, dressed in beige chinos and a navy polo shirt tucked tightly into his trousers, which accentuated his food-lover's waistline.

He was a confident man because *he* started the questioning, straight after Ruppert and Bonnet had told him who they were and explained that they were trying to find out the fate of the missing Monsieur Max.

'Any theories, Inspector?'

'It's Commandant, Monsieur Rachet, and, if you don't mind, we'll ask the questions.'

'Sorry. No offence. Fire away. Shoot.'

'First, give me a flavour of who he is. I know you've been his regular taxi driver for a few years. What's he like?'

'Honestly? I don't feel that I really know him. The truth? I wouldn't want him as a friend. You're in a strange position in the front seat of a taxi. You know where your passengers are going and how often they go there. You know, sometimes, who they're going there with, because they're also in the cab. But, if you're a good driver, you're like a priest or a counsellor, you let them talk, unless you're a garrulous gobshite like the ones who never shut up about themselves. Me, I like to listen . . .'

'Is that right, Monsieur Rachet?'

'Franck, please. Call me Franck. Sure I'm a listener! I'm sat there up front like a sponge just taking in everything he says. He's telling me one minute how so-and-so is a very attractive woman he likes a lot who he thinks is interested in him, but he has to be careful because her husband is a right bastard, and then the next minute he's telling me he thinks she's a right pain because she doesn't like him seeing anybody else despite the fact that she's only free at certain times because her old man keeps her on a tight rein. Then he tells me what he thinks of everyone who does any work for him, like the plumber is a fat, smelly slob who doesn't know his arse from his ball-cock. Next he'll go on about how he wishes he could settle down, but women can't be trusted further than you can throw them. Him, saying that! He rants about his ex-wives so much, I actually thought he might have had seven of them all on the go at the same time, like he's a Mormon or something.'

'OK, OK, thanks, Franck, you've been very . . . frank,' said Ruppert and then, turning to Bonnet who was holding his pen static over his notebook, added, 'Did you get all that, Lieutenant?'

'Was I talking too fast?' asked Rachet.

'Not at all,' Ruppert assured him, 'but tell me who the most recent conquests were and where they lived.'

'Lucille something – I never knew her last name – she's

his regular squeeze over near Les Baux. Big swanky *mas* in huge grounds with wonderful views. Pool, tennis court, mini-golf, all the trimmings. She's bored out of her bra according to Monsieur Max. Some kind of English actress of a certain age, you know – she's the one with the bastard of a husband. Then, before that, there was Melanie over at Eygalières. I don't know where she lived, he always met her for lunch at Sous les Micocouliers restaurant just off the main drag and he'd tell me, "It's not a wait and return, Franck, so make yourself scarce. I'll call you if I need you." '

'Was she married too?'

'Oh my god, yes. That's a story. She's not married any more. Separated. Her husband found out about Max and went ballistic. He painted the gates in big red letters with the word . . .'

'. . . Adulterer?'

'That's it. I suppose Gérard told you?'

'Not who did it. How do you know?'

'Monsieur Max. He told me, but I was to keep it to myself, which was difficult, a story like that . . . and this is a small town. The Monsieur was livid. He asked me if I knew anyone who could be paid to work the man over for him.'

'What did you say?'

'I told him not to be so daft and to count himself lucky to get off so lightly. I wouldn't have just painted his gates, I can tell you, I'd have shoved his head where the sun don't shine.'

'Well thanks, Franck. I appreciate your . . . candour. Before you go, when was the last time you saw him?'

'I looked up the last job I did, after Gérard rang me asking if I'd seen him. I took him to Glanum. He said he wanted to see what further excavations they'd been doing. He was keen on all that Roman business and would go on his walks on the Via Domitia and bore me silly with all the history.'

'When exactly was this?'

'The tenth of last month. It was a Wednesday because I can remember thinking he usually keeps market days free. Never misses one when he's here does our Monsieur Max. I was the one who gave him that name, by the way, and it just kind of stuck.'

'What time did he leave Glanum?'

'He didn't leave with me. That's just it. He said he'd walk back. I don't know when he left or what happened to him after that as I haven't heard from him, or seen him, since.'

'Thanks, Monsieur Rachet. We'll call you if we need you. You've been very . . . enlightening.'

*   *   *

Ruppert and Bonnet watched Rachet march to his car, reverse out with another crunch on the gravel, and speed off.

'What did you make of him, sir?'

'He painted a picture for us.'

'Do you believe he could really just sit quietly in the front of his cab just speaking when he's spoken to, allowing the passenger to talk and not interrupt?'

'No . . . but he expected us to take him at his word. We can never do that in this game, Bonnet.'

'What now, sir? It's just that I'd like to polish off some paperwork at the gendarmerie if that's OK with you, so that I can be free of it for tomorrow.'

'Yes, that's fine. I'll finish up here and lock up. I can walk back into town. I'm going to pick the brains, as you would say, of another estate agent – my friend Philippe – who'll know all about Sam Rodgers and Monsieur Max. Tomorrow morning, can you pick me up at Hotel Gounod at nine thirty? My wife and I will be having breakfast there.'

'Certainly, sir. See you then.'

Ruppert returned various papers to the study and sat making some notes of his thoughts so far and running through some questions in his head for Philippe.

As he got up to leave, he noticed a leather document folder by the desk – curious that he hadn't noticed it before. It was very light, as if nothing was in it, but opening it up he found yet another file which turned out to contain both an English and a French will for Clive Maximilian Collins – that's where the Max comes from, he realised. Perhaps his wife could translate the English one for him. He put them, the book and his other papers into his briefcase and left the house.

3.

As he walked up Chemin de Figuières Folles, then along Avenue Albert Gleizes onto Avenue Fauconnet, Ruppert was thinking that he didn't really like Monsieur Max.

Then again, could he trust the view of the guardian and a taxi driver? How do people talk of their bosses? Is it ever polite? Isn't it a case of kicking them when they're down because that's the only time people in their position can?

Tomorrow, he'd try and interview Sam Rodgers, Melanie Beauvais and, if they could get hold of her, Lucille Lamb – the actress whose name and number Gérard had written down for them earlier. He'd then also need to speak to the son in London, try and find out a bit more about the ex-wives, perhaps, and maybe fit in seeing Taval. A busy day or two in prospect.

Only distracted on his walk by the music of the children's carousel in the Place de la République, he was sitting, before he knew it, on the little terrace outside the Café des Arts with Philippe, who was as smiling and debonair as always, with a drink in front of him.

'What'll you have, Jules? I'm having an Aperol spritz.'

'What's that when it's at home?'

'Jules, Jules, I give up. It's an uber trendy Italian drink, a bit like campari, with prosecco.'

'But we're French, Philippe. Do the Italians drink our pastis?'

'So, what's it to be, Jules, something old or something new?'

'A pastis Janot if they have it, please.'

After ordering, Philippe asked, 'To what do I owe the pleasure of your company for an aperitif this evening, my friend?'

'I want to ask you about Clive Collins and the property he bought from Sam Rodgers in Figuières Folles. What can you tell me?'

'Crikey, Jules, that's going back a bit.'

'Ten years, in fact.'

'Well, it stays in my mind because I still see both of them from time to time around the town, or I did until Monsieur Collins went missing.'

'How often do you see Rodgers?'

'He still comes back once or twice every year, at least. He regrets selling the house, that's for sure. He was forced into it by financial difficulties at the time, but, you know, there was a funny option clause he insisted on being inserted in the contract and even the notaire wasn't very happy about it. Rodgers wanted to have the right of first refusal if and when the house was next for sale.'

'Is that usual?'

'Let's put it this way, that's the only case *I* know of. I'm not saying it hasn't been done in other instances, but it must be a rarity.'

'Was Rodgers difficult about the sale then?'

'Almost impossible. I had to warn Collins not to antagonise him in any way if he wanted it to happen at all. There were times Rodgers threatened to take it off the market. He was extremely awkward over everything, including arguing the toss about the value of furniture and other piddling items. Collins nearly gave up, but, mind you, he's equally stubborn. In the end I think *his* stubborn determination won, if you like, and Rodgers still seems to harbour a grudge, although at one million euros it was a great sale for him.'

'Was there a cash element in the deal, dare I ask? Look, that isn't part of my enquiries, I hasten to add.'

'As it's you, Jules, let's say I have my suspicions. Rodgers was certainly keen for me to ask for it as a condition of selling to Collins. He wanted fifty thousand euros, but I told him to leave me out of it and, if he was determined to go down that route, he'd better speak to Collins himself. I could lose my job over something like that.'

'Is that what he did?'

'I don't know, but Rodgers insisted on using a notaire

he'd found in Tarascon, not our usual one in Avignon which annoyed me. During the signing ceremony, just before signature, the notaire – a chap as old as the hills – asked me to have a word with him outside his office. It was something he and Rodgers had arranged, I was sure about that, because when he got outside he asked whether I thought Collins had understood everything, as his French didn't seem to be very good. That was a ruse because Collins, although he always speaks to me in English, could speak a bit of French and, as the notaire jolly well knew, I'd given Collins an English translation so there were no worries on that score. When we went back in, Rodgers nodded at the notaire and they went ahead and signed.'

'What? And nobody said anything? I heard that used to happen all the time, but I thought it had died out.'

'It still happens, less so now. Sellers can fiddle some tax, but savvy buyers know they can never claim it in any future capital gains tax computation of theirs when they come to sell. Collins was happy to get the place, but something rankled with him, I could tell, so I think he must have ended up paying the extra cash. If I ever saw him in town and I'd had a sighting of Rodgers, I'd say, "Rodgers is in town, have you seen him?" and he'd reply, impersonating Rodgers' regional accent, "Why doesn't he bugger off back to Birmingham?" '

'What did you make of each of them?'

'They're clients, Jules, I don't have to go on holiday

with them. I'm sorry Collins has disappeared and I hope he's still alive, but the fact you're involved suggests you lot think otherwise. He's got a reputation locally as a bit of a womaniser – unlikely I know – I always took that with a pinch of salt. He's outwardly charming, but it doesn't fool me. I'm an estate agent, after all – I can do charm as easily as the next charlatan – and, as they say, you can't bullshit a bullshitter.'

'Do you know of anyone who would want to see him out of the way?'

'Other than me, because I could then sell his house? No, not really.'

'Don't put ideas into my head, Philippe. What about Rodgers, what do you make of him?'

'Him? Well . . . I've never been sure. He's always been very vague about his background. He's an author, you know . . . of crime books. He's now very popular, he tells me, and he carps that if he'd had the success a year or two earlier, he never would have sold the house. That's become like a mantra whenever I see him. He's quite aggressive and I started to think that his books might be a bit more based on fact than fiction, but that's my own creative imagination working overtime, I suspect.'

'When did you last see either Collins or Rodgers?'

'Not sure about Collins. I was so used to seeing him that it's all a bit subconscious and with his vanishing act, I'm not even sure when I stopped seeing him in the town.'

'What about Rodgers?'

'A few weeks ago, I think?'

'Really?'

'Not now you've said that. It may have been months ago. You don't really think about things like that unless you're put on the spot and asked to be specific. A few weeks ago, but I couldn't swear to it.'

'I'm planning on interviewing Rodgers tomorrow, Philippe. I won't even say I know you, but thanks for the insights. If you think of anything else about either of them, let me know. I'll pay for the drinks, it's the least I can do, even if you did have the nerve to neck some Italian muck.'

'Cheers,' said Philippe, 'any time. Let me know how it goes.'

*   *   *

Ruppert walked home. Inside, going up the stone stairs to the first floor kitchen, the smells told him he would be having brandade de morue de Nîmes, an all-year-round favourite of his. He was already grateful his wife hadn't taken him up on his earlier suggestion of something cold.

Madame Ruppert had a Django Reinhardt CD playing and a chilled glass of Cassis white ready for him.

'Perfect, chérie,' he said. 'Can't think of a better way to end the day.'

'Start the evening, I think you mean,' she replied. 'Sit down, Jules. I'll serve it right up and you can tell me what you've been up to.'

'How about *your* afternoon first?'

'It was dull. The town hall is not the place for excitement. I was so bored that at one point I looked up the file for Clive Collins. Did you know there was an enquiry about him trying to bribe an official over planning permission?'

'What happened?'

'Nothing. The complaint wasn't upheld for lack of evidence. "Another bribe," Claudine said, when I discussed it with her.'

'Who was the official at the time?'

'The younger of the Taval brothers. You know, the older one has that plumbing and heating business in Eyragues.'

'He's the one who did the work on the pool. Fancy that. Fascinating! I've often thought you'd be better at my job than I am. Maybe we should do a swap?'

'And anytime you want to take over cooking duties, just tell me.'

'You're better at that too, fortunately for me.'

Madame Ruppert put the plate in front of him with a slightly smug smile.

'I want you to help me out with this case a bit more,

actually,' he said. 'I'd like you to read a book in English for me, if you can bear to, and see if it reveals anything about the author, Sam Rodgers, who used to live in the house before Monsieur Collins. *And,*' he continued, 'can you have a quick look at his English will for me sometime and tell me the main provisions?'

'How exciting,' she said. 'That'll save me from the television.'

After supper, she asked, 'Why don't we go for a stroll. You can show me the Collins house and, on our way back, we can have an ice cream from Un Été in Rue Lafayette and take a turn round the town.

*   *   *

They were soon at the house, and Ruppert was puzzled.

'This is the house. That's odd. I must have left the outside lights on when I left.'

'You surely didn't switch them *on* by accident as you left did you?'

'I don't think so,' said Ruppert, pushing the buzzer by the gates. Maybe Gérard is here.'

'Who's Gérard? The caretaker?'

'Yes, sort of, that's right,' and, fumbling in his pockets,

he said, 'Blast! I've left the keys at home. I'll ring Gérard on his mobile, if we can't get an answer here.'

With no answer to repeated buzzing, Ruppert rang Gérard. Getting no reply, he turned to his wife and said, 'Come on, he's obviously not here or else we would have heard his phone ringing, wouldn't we? It'll have to wait until tomorrow. The place is not going to come to any harm.'

They turned to walk up Rue Camille Pelletan which took them straight back to the centre of town.

'What's Gérard like?' asked Madame Ruppert. 'Is he under suspicion?'

'I haven't ruled anybody out, but it's early days. I'm not sure about him. He seems straightforward, but there are a few things that trouble me. And, as to a motive, I haven't come up with one yet.'

They stopped for their ice creams, a violet cornet for him and a tub of sea-salted caramel for her. They ambled back, watching the boys skateboarding outside the town hall in Place Pelissier.

Once back in their house with the washing up done and the news watched, he said that if she didn't mind, he'd go up to bed and read.

'Fall asleep, more like,' she said. 'I'll stay up for a bit and take a look at that book for you.'

*   *   *

The Rupperts had ordered their breakfasts on the tiny outside terrace of the Hotel Gounod, tucked in the corner of the Place de la République. It had just arrived, a simple assemblage of orange juice, fresh fruit, croissants, bread, butter, apricot jam and fresh coffee – his favourite start to the day.

'Don't you want to know what I found in the book?' she asked.

'You know I do. I've asked several times and you know perfectly well you've kept me on tenterhooks saying I'd have to wait until we were having breakfast. What did you make of it?'

'Well, for a start, it's set in St Rémy and Avignon. You would have seen that for yourself if you'd bothered to flick through the pages. It's gruesome – some very nasty business in it. Three deaths so far, and I'm only on page seventy-five.'

'What's it about?'

'As far as I can tell it's about revenge, and it's full of witchcraft and weird religious rites. Quite unpleasant actually.'

'Oh, I see, well nothing like this case then.'

'There is one thing. The murders so far have all involved water.'

'How do you mean? Drownings?'

'Yes – bodies found in the rivers and canals of Avignon, you know in that rough area where those little watermills are that we only go to when the Festival is on.'

'And, in the next chapter, I bet someone will get pushed off the Pont d'Avignon by the little chapel of St Nicholas.'

'Don't mock. It's research. It might turn up something, so I'll persevere with it. It's well written, actually, even if it is quite disturbing. I'd bear that in mind when you meet the author.'

They'd just about finished breakfast when Ruppert reached for his briefcase and said, 'I nearly forgot. Can you take a look at this English will for me whilst I look at the French one?'

He produced the wills and handed one over to his wife. She read through it quickly, her eyes moving down the page.

'It's authentic, in the same sort of language our own wills are in. Of course, there's no wife mentioned – I assume he's been married, because there's a mention of the son, Stephen Baker – not Collins, notice – inheriting a flat in London, but also something about him having use of the house in France for a month a year for as long as it is owned by the beneficiary, who is . . . Monsieur . . . wait for it . . . Gérard Paquet – that's the guardian, right? All of the money in investments and all other accounts is to go to the son, apart from a list of about five women who get small bequests and the right to choose anything as a souvenir from the house in France. How strange.'

'Are you positive? Read it again, please, just to make sure.'

Ruppert had just finished reading the short French will and was still shaking his head when she confirmed that, 'Yes, it's like I said, Gérard Paquet gets the house and the son gets the money and use of the house for any month of his choice each year.'

'The French will says pretty much the same thing although it's just dealing with property held in France – the house going to Gérard and all the money in the French bank account going to his son.'

'Do you think Gérard knows? What a turn-up!'

'This is a bit of a bombshell, I'll give you that. It'll make my next interview with Gérard interesting, that's for sure. He hasn't mentioned that he stands to inherit the house, but in this game it isn't ever that obvious. It would be too cut and dried if it were. I've got to be careful even thinking this gives a motive, as Collins isn't actually dead as far as we know. Gérard probably does know all about the wills – he's nosy enough to have found them.'

As they were finishing their breakfasts, Bonnet arrived.

'Monsieur, Madame. I'm not too early am I? I know you said nine thirty and it's only nine fifteen. I can wait in the car if you like.'

'No, don't worry, Lieutenant, I must run along to the town hall, so I'd better be off,' said Madame Ruppert.

With that she left and, after Bonnet had declined a

coffee and Ruppert had paid the bill, they set off for the Château des Alpilles, in the direction of Tarascon.

'Just swing by the Collins house, please, Bonnet. I want to check something.'

They were soon there.

'What is it, boss?' asked Bonnet.

'I may have left the lights on.'

He was soon back in the car.

'No, nothing on and nothing open. Perhaps there's a faulty sensor. I'll check with Gérard when we next see him.'

They went back to the main road and got themselves onto the Route du Rougadou that led to the Château des Alpilles.

Ruppert told Bonnet about the contents of the will, which stunned him.

'Why didn't Gérard say something?'

'Maybe he doesn't know.'

'I find that hard to believe.'

They were soon driving down the tree-lined drive leading to the hotel. Some of the guests were still at breakfast as they arrived and they all looked up to see who it was. Bonnet dropped Ruppert off at the front and went to park the car.

Ruppert knew the owner and she came over to him.

'Hello, Jules. I suppose this is an official visit?'

'Yes, but informal. We want to have a chat with one of your guests, Monsieur Rodgers. We thought we might find him sitting out here. Has he had room service?'

'No, he prefers to take breakfast by the pool. Quite the swimmer, I believe.'

Bonnet came over to where they stood and, as he approached, Ruppert led his colleague in the direction of the pool, remembering as they walked that there was a very deep reservoir at the rear of the hotel filled with large Koi carp. More water, he thought.

As they neared the outside swimming pool, sure enough, there was one person, in the full glare of the sun, sitting in Vilebrequin trunks and tucking into a plateful of croissants. They both knew that he was the person they were looking for and went over to introduce themselves.

'What's this all about? I only arrived here yesterday. Is this part of the reception committee?'

'Your French is very good, Monsieur,' Ruppert replied.

'An immersion course in Avignon, but never mind that. How can I help you gentlemen?'

'It's just that I know you sold a house here in St Rémy to Monsieur Collins.'

'Well. What of it? That was at least ten years ago.'

'It's just that he has disappeared. You left a message for him, we're following that up and hoping you can give us some background.'

'Disappeared? Well I never. I see him when I come back to town. He doesn't like it, I know that, but I've got the hide of an elephant and, hey, I quite like winding him up. He knows, of course, that I regretted selling the house.'

'And you want it back? There's a clause in the sale and purchase agreement to that effect, isn't there?'

'You boys *have* done your homework, haven't you? I wouldn't read too much into that if I were you. I said I was sorry to be selling it at the time and I put an option in place so I felt I hadn't lost it forever. But I like to annoy him. I don't know if I would ever exercise the option, even if it came to it.'

'You're an author, aren't you?' asked Ruppert.

'A policeman who reads books, whatever next,' replied Rodgers. 'They've been translated into French – all ten of them – and they sell well over here. I'd probably buy a bigger place than Collins has, to be honest. Anyway, I like staying in places like this. And why not?'

'When did you last see Collins?'

'Wait a minute ... that would be just before Christmas, I think. Bumped into him having dinner in Découverte. I was on my own. He wasn't. Needless to say he didn't ask me to join them.'

'Who was he with?'

'I didn't know her and I didn't get introduced. Attractive though.'

'When did you arrive in St Rémy?'

'Like I said, I arrived here yesterday. I've come for the Festival.'

'How long are you staying?'

'Not sure yet. Maybe three weeks, maybe more. Depends

how the writing goes. I'm working on a book set in the Camargue. That's an area full of mystery, if you ask me.'

'You would tell me, Monsieur, if there were any difficulties between you and Collins, wouldn't you?' Ruppert asked.

'Look. I'll be honest with you and that's without a lawyer present. I don't like him, but as to why he's disappeared, I haven't a clue. Probably with some woman somewhere.'

'Did you ever fall out about money?'

'How do you mean? I never had any dealings with him, not since selling him the house.'

'Was there a cash element to it, perhaps?'

'Good God, no. I'd never do anything like that in a million years. Too scared of you lot. Anyway, I used to be a lawyer, so I always follow the letter of the law.'

'Thank you, Monsieur. That's all for now. And we know where to find you, after all.'

As they left, Rodgers stood, walked over to the pool and slid himself in, to cool himself off. Bonnet and Ruppert walked back to the main building of the hotel and went up the stairs through the doubled-doored entrance. Reception was at the back of an elegantly furnished hall.

'Ah, Jules. I take it you found him?'

'Yes, thanks. Can you confirm when he arrived please?'

'Yesterday at midday, because we kept his bags until his room was ready. He arrived by a local taxi, which was the only thing that struck me as slightly strange.'

As they were leaving the grounds in the car, Bonnet

turned to Ruppert and said, 'Eygalières?'

'Yes, to see Madame Beauvais.'

'We're meeting some nice characters, boss, aren't we.'

'You're in the wrong job, Bonnet, if you want that, or if you want to win friends and influence people. Rodgers is a tough nut and he gave nothing away. Letter of the law indeed. That, and his use of the word "honest", confirmed to me that he took an under-the-table cash payment when he sold the house. Who knows what else he's capable of? Madame is reading one of his books for me, a murder mystery. I think he's *her* number one suspect.'

'What about you, Commandant? Do you think he had a hand in the disappearance of Monsieur Max?'

'Not unless it's a double bluff. He, like Gérard, seems a bit too elementary a solution. I wish solving all crime was that easy.'

'Maybe both of them did it, sir?'

'Did what, Bonnet? We haven't got a body yet. Until we do, this is still a missing person case. Let's see what our estate agent in Eygalières can say about that. I'm just going to ring that actress Gérard mentioned, to see if we can meet her this afternoon. You can find out how it feels to have more than one woman on the go at the same time, Bonnet.'

Ruppert rang the number.

'Lucille Lamb?'

'Yes?'

'Do you speak French?'

'Yes. I've been coming to France for ever and I'm married to a French rock star so of course I speak fluent French. And I'm an actress so I used a voice coach to get the accent right.'

'Thank you, Madame, for that. I am Commandant Ruppert and, with my colleague Lieutenant Bonnet, we are investigating the disappearance of Monsieur Clive Collins. We would like to come and talk to you this afternoon, if that is convenient, around two thirty?'

'Yes, poor Max. If you want to see me, it will have to be today as my husband is back tomorrow and I wouldn't want to talk about this when he's around.'

'We may need to see him.'

'I doubt he can help with your enquiries, Commandant.'

'We'll see you this afternoon, Madame. Goodbye.' Ruppert put his phone back into his pocket. 'Well, Bonnet, that's fixed. I'll treat you to lunch on the way there from Eygalières.'

'Thank you. By the way, sir, what did she mean at the hotel when she said Rodgers had arrived in a local taxi?'

'Don't know. I'm sure she's used to seeing Nîmes or Avignon taxis arriving. Perhaps Rodgers uses a local firm or maybe she was hinting he'd arrived in St Rémy earlier than he was admitting. We'll see.'

4.

They drove back into St Rémy, then around its one way system of boulevards, before leaving the town. Ruppert could never get enough of the tree-lined roads that spread like tentacles in all directions from the centre, and the drive to Eygalières was a treat to be enjoyed whatever the purpose.

With the Alpilles to the right, visible through the plane trees supposedly planted on the orders of Napoleon, the long Avenue de la Libération was a really splendid way in or out of the town. Ruppert, along with everyone else, liked to think that the Emperor himself was responsible for this natural and lasting legacy, but he had his doubts.

The countryside looked particularly beautiful and he and his wife often enjoyed a drive to Eygalières on its market day, because it was so much more civilised than the crowded scrum of St Rémy's own.

It was a sleepy village and Ruppert loved its

time-stood-still quality. They parked easily enough, right outside Agence Maison Lux in the main street.

Madame Beauvais had her desk right in the window and, with a see-and-be-seen air about her, waved to them as they got out of the car.

'Nice to see you, gentlemen. I thought you might be police when you rang to arrange to meet me,' was how she greeted them as they walked in and introduced themselves.

'Céline, you can pop out and have your coffee break now if you like. I'll look after these two,' she said to the only other occupant of the office.

When her assistant had left, Madame Beauvais turned to them and asked, 'Now I suppose you've come to talk about Max?'

Realising they'd lost the element of surprise, they took the two seats offered in front of her desk. She was a disconcertingly attractive dark-haired woman, probably in her early fifties, and Bonnet was correct about the fluttering eyelids.

'When did you last see him, Madame?' asked Ruppert.

'Last year, to break it off. He'd already cost me my marriage. We had lunch here in Eygalières. It was very traumatic for me, but he just took it in his stride. "If that's how you feel, then that's it, it's over. Your loss," is about all he said.'

'Were you separated from your husband by then?'

'Yes, I was. I'm sure you know about the graffiti and all

that. My husband had found out about the affair and he went crazy, as all French men do. It's all right for them to play the field and we're meant to put up with it, but it's different when it's the other way round. It doesn't help that this village is small and even with so many Parisian second home-owners, it seems everyone knows everyone else's business. We had a row, of course, for what seemed like a whole day. In the end, he stormed out and, as I later found out, he drove to St Rémy to have it out with Max. Fortunately for them both, Max wasn't at home, otherwise I'm not sure what René would have done. He had some paint in the car and, well, you know the rest.'

'Is your husband a violent man, Madame?'

'Well, he's had his moments, but, no, he's not violent. I was usually the one who threw things if we had an argument. He can be so frustrating.'

'What do you think has happened to Monsieur Max?'

'It wouldn't surprise me if something in his past has caught up with him. Not that I hold anything against him – I finished with him, remember – actually, he did me a favour. I was glad to be out of my marriage, but I knew I could never stay with a man quite as deceitful as Max. It took me a long time to realise it as he can be so charming, but little by little, I came to realise what sort of man he truly is.'

'And what's that?' was Bonnet's first question.

'A complete bloody conman, a man who takes advantage of women, that's what. It doesn't work as a lasting technique. Remember that, Lieutenant.'

With Bonnet suitably abashed, Ruppert had one more question.

'Did you or your husband have anything to do with the disappearance of Monsieur Max?'

'I knew you'd ask me that. *I* certainly didn't. I don't wish him any harm even if I'm glad he's out of my life. He can go and mess up other people's for all I care.'

'What about your husband?'

'René? You must be joking. He might have punched Max on the nose if he ever saw him again, but you know what he did when he moved out of our home? He moved straight in with his girlfriend who lives round the corner. I still see him, naturally. It's hard not to. But we agreed to divorce. He looks happy enough, so he probably realised that Max had done him a favour, once he calmed down and his floozy sorted out his wounded pride. Men, pah!'

'Where would we find Réne, Madame?'

Madame Beauvais looked at her watch.

'Now? At the Café du Centre, talking about football with his fellow builders. I'll walk you across and introduce you to him if you like. That will give everyone something else to talk about.'

'Thank you, Madame, that would be helpful.'

Ruppert and Bonnet were soon standing to the side of the café talking to a very surprised René Beauvais who had sheepishly stood up and walked over from his table – watched by his mates – when summoned by the woman who was still his wife.

'I'm embarrassed about the whole episode, Monsieur,' René said when asked about the graffiti. 'It was in the heat of the moment. I don't know what came over me.'

'You must see how it looks,' explained Ruppert. 'You've shown aggression to a man who subsequently disappears. What are we to make of that?'

'It looks bad, I know, but I never actually got to see him, and the following day it all seemed like a dream. I never even attempted to look for him after that. It was all over. I'm perfectly happy. My work is going well, doing up house after house, and my new relationship is better than the one I had with Melanie. You've got to believe me.'

'Bonnet, take down Monsieur Beauvais' details. We may need to contact him again.'

As they drove back to St Rémy, Bonnet asked Ruppert what he made of all that.

'The trouble is, Bonnet, when you've been in the job as long as I have, you reach the point where you don't believe a single word anybody says. I'm sure she can be manipulative, there's no doubt about that, but she clearly met her match in Max. I'm not sure she was the one who broke it off, so there may be some resentment there. Who knows? . . . René? . . . He seems harmless enough even if, as I suspect, he can be a bit of a hothead. As for planning a disappearance or murder, which I'm increasingly thinking it is, he hasn't got it in him. She, on the other hand, who knows? Thanks to her intuition, she had time to plan exactly what she would say to us.'

*   *   *

Ruppert and Bonnet both enjoyed their al fresco lunch at the Bistrot du Paradou. "Heaven on earth" best described the lunch and the place, according to Bonnet. Ruppert was glad the experience wasn't wasted on his young colleague and pleased that the plat du jour, the volaille de Bresse that particular day, had hit the spot for both of them.

'On to the next round then,' said Ruppert when they were back in the car and driving up towards Les Baux. 'I wonder what we'll make of Lucille Lamb?'

Franck Rachet hadn't been exaggerating. The *mas* was set in beautiful grounds against a backdrop of the rocky Alpilles, with stunning views of the mountain-top village of Les Baux.

The beauty didn't stop there, for Lucille Lamb was a blonde who knew how to present herself at her best. A notch up even from Melanie Beauvais. Ruppert was beginning to see things a little from Max's point of view. That is, until she spoke. It wasn't how she said it, but what she said and her absorption with herself – the me, me, me. All attractiveness fell away like you were looking at the picture of Dorian Gray. Her answer to how long she had known Max was a long one, carefully rehearsed, Ruppert suspected, almost learnt off by heart.

'Max and I met in London when I was at drama college and we lived together in a tiny, tiny flat in the centre, which you could do quite cheaply in those days. He worked in advertising then, although he was desperate to have something, anything, to do with showbiz. He became a producer and set up a talent agency as he called it, trying to be all Hollywood. Inevitably, we went our separate ways when I was on tour and our relationship just fizzled out. There was no closure as such so, from time to time, we rekindled it and picked up where we left off, especially if we were between jobs, between lovers, or just bored. He was married a couple of times, so was I, but that didn't ever stop us enjoying an on-off affair like an itch that has to be scratched. Am I boring you?'

She had noticed that she had lost her audience when she noticed the bored faces of Ruppert and Bonnet looking more at each other than at her.

'Not at all, Madame.'

'For heaven's sake, call me Lucille.'

'OK, Lucille, when did you last see Monsieur Max?'

'Well, my husband has been here off and on this year, so not much recently. We had a great summer last year when Jacques was on tour with his band, but Max was two-timing me then, the cheat, with that Eygalières tart of his. Some days, get this, he'd take her off to Saintes Marie de la Mer and then he'd come back and whisk me off to Oustau de Beaumanière, just up the road. He only enjoys taking me to places where I'm known, saying, "We can hide in plain sight, Lucille. Don't worry. What's wrong with two old friends catching up over dinner? Who cares what people make of it?" But he hasn't ever taken *me* to the Camargue, where nobody knows us at all and there's no one to show off to. He's like that.'

'Is your husband jealous of Max?'

'Who told you that? Never mind, I've always played that up with Max to test him, but Jacques is too chilled to be concerned. I'd feed Max stories about being kept under lock and key by an extremely possessive husband. Max likes courting danger; I think it excites him. He came to believe my husband's a monster and was sorry for me.'

'Does your husband actually know about Max?'

'Not really about the naughty bits. He might know, I suppose, but he always laughs about him and really just knows him as an old friend of mine. We never socialise all together. His joke name for Max is "your ex en Provence". Funny, isn't it?'

'Why didn't you want us to talk about this in front of your husband then?'

'I didn't know what you were going to say, did I? I don't want to risk any kind of big reveal. I love my husband,

Commandant, and I rather like our life here too much to want to risk it all, especially as Max has disappeared. That would be ridiculous. Like throwing it all away, and, for what?'

'What do you think's happened to Max?'

'Shacked up with somebody, like that estate agency bint, or lying low somewhere maybe.'

'We might need to talk to your husband.'

'Don't tell him anything more than he needs to know, please, I'm begging you, for the sake of my marriage.'

'I can't promise you anything, Madame.'

'Can I offer you two a drink? I know it's early, but it's six o'clock somewhere, as Jacques always says.'

'No thank you. We've got further enquiries to make on the missing Monsieur Max. Thanks for your time.'

As the two policemen went to the car, Ruppert turned to Bonnet.

'I'll drive, Lieutenant. I want to go back the other way, which is more interesting, past the stone quarries, you know, the Cathédrale d'Images place where they have the Picasso and Van Gogh light shows.'

As they drove, Bonnet asked the inevitable question.

'What did you make of Lucille Lamb?'

'I was thinking that maybe she and Max deserve each other.'

'She *was* full of herself, wasn't she? As for her calling *Melanie* a tart. How about that?'

'What did you think of her saying her husband was so

chilled that he wouldn't care and then telling us that she had made up all the jealousy stuff that caused Rachet to say Max thought him a right bastard?'

'Deliberately putting us off the scent, perhaps?'

'Could be. That means we'll have to see him for ourselves.'

'Did you mean it, sir, when you said you couldn't promise not to tell him about their affair?'

'I don't know, Bonnet. I'm here to find out if there's a dead man out there, not to act as a marriage counsellor. In all this we're here to protect the dead, so to speak, not the living. And, sometimes, it pays to get some people a bit on edge.'

They drove on round the twisting roads of the Alpilles, through the pine forests on either side that were punctuated with rocky outcrops.

'Bonnet, see if you can ring Taval, the plumber. You'll find his number in the file in my briefcase.'

*   *   *

Bonnet was forceful on the phone and, prompted by Ruppert, had insisted that Taval be at the Collins house in thirty minutes.

At the house, Ruppert asked Bonnet to call on the neighbours, mainly the house next door but also the large house opposite, which had its back to the Collins residence and its front entrance on the main road. Those seemed to Ruppert to be the only properties whose windows gave a clear outlook onto Max's gates and garden.

More or less by the time he had opened up the house, Taval had arrived in his beat-up old Renault van and Ruppert went back outside to meet him.

'I don't like coming back to this place, Monsieur. There was always something going wrong, not all of it down to me.'

'I want to ask you about Collins, Monsieur Taval.'

'Georges, please.'

'When did you last see him?'

'Well, I *didn't* see him, did I? I came one day last month and he wasn't here as we'd arranged. I gave Gérard a mouthful about that. This ruddy leak of his – I want it sorted and I want my money. These Brits think they can take liberties. Not with me, they can't.'

'I understand you can be tough with people who don't pay up.'

'Who told you that? Well, what would you do if you didn't get paid when you'd done the work? How would you feel?'

'You didn't do anything drastic with Monsieur Collins, did you?'

'You must be joking. He's way too slippery for that. Always talking about having the lawyers on me. If I'd touched him, he'd have had me in court in no time at all.'

'So when did you last see him?'

'At the start of the year. That's when this leak problem started after one of the frosts. He wasn't keeping the pool ticking over like I told him to, and he blamed me. *He* caused it, but I'd been trying to get the final instalment out of him for the pool for months and months and he kept refusing, saying the pattern of the tiles was all wrong. Rubbish. He designed it, not me. When he had the leak, he then changed tack, saying he'd pay me in full if the leak was fixed. The cheek of it. Finally, after making him sweat for a bit, I said I'd be there. Then, when I turned up, blow me he wasn't even at home and I'm still out of pocket and none the wiser.'

'Didn't your brother, Christian, have a spot of bother with him a while back over planning?'

'You'll have to ask him yourself about the details. I'd heard about it, but Christian said he couldn't discuss it. Confidential it was, but Collins once said to me, "You Taval brothers are both the same." I asked him what he meant by that and he just shrugged. I let it go, otherwise I would have hit him.'

'Are you a violent man?'

'No, I'm not. I've got a heart problem, so I've calmed down a bit. Now, on doctor's orders, I count to ten before I react in case I respond as I would have done years ago.'

OK, thanks, Monsieur Taval. I'll be in touch if needs be.'

'Anytime, but, if you don't mind, I have a question for you. It's this. What am I supposed to do about my money?'

'If I were you, I'd fix the leak – you can ring Gérard to make a time – and then you'll have to send a final invoice, assuming there was an original one?'

'There *is* an invoice. That's something Collins is good at. Everything has to be invoiced by me and paid by cheque from him. I shouldn't be telling you this, but that's not what most people try and do, but I need my books straight and it's paid off in this case. I just hope I get my money in the end. It's hit me hard and I'm seriously out of pocket over that pool.'

Taval drove off, the diesel of his van leaving a smelly legacy.

Bonnet returned to find Ruppert still standing in the garden by the pool.

'How did that go? I saw Taval leaving.'

'He tells me he's a reformed character. Not the man he was thanks to a heart condition and he now avoids confrontation. Or so he says. And he wouldn't be drawn about a planning dispute his brother, Christian, had with Collins which Madame Ruppert told me about. We'll have to see the brother some time.'

'Interesting. I wonder if they were in cahoots about putting some pressure on Collins?'

'We'll have to find out. How did you get on with the neighbours?'

'They'll see you tomorrow. They can't wait to find out what we think has happened to our Max. The couple next door, Monsieur and Madame Sim, started telling me about the "comings and goings next door" until I told them to save it until they saw you. Then Madame du Perry, in the big house there, was quite snooty about Collins and said she didn't have much to do with him. I don't think we'll get much out of them, but you never know.'

'Thanks, Bonnet. I'll just write up a few notes and then go home. You can shoot off now if you like and I'll see you tomorrow, back here at the same sort of time.'

When he'd finished, Ruppert locked the doors and gates and walked up through the town. On his way home, he called in at Joël Durand's to pick up a bar of his wife's favourite, a dark chocolate and cardamom, and popped across the road for an evening baguette from La Folie du Pain. Then, thinking he'd be helpful, he walked to Place Hilaire and La Cave aux Fromages to pick up some cheeses for supper.

He arrived home at the same time as his wife and when they were upstairs in the kitchen, he showed her his purchases.

'I thought we'd have bread and cheese tonight, unless you've got other plans for supper?'

'No, that's a lovely idea – even if you did choose the cheeses without me – something simple to eat and then I can get on with reading *Assassin*. You set it all out on the table and I'll get us a drink. What shall we have?

'How about that nice bottle of red, the Domaine des Terres Blanches?'

'Perfect.'

5.

Having been regaled over breakfast with the lurid storyline of *Assassin* and the details of several more watery deaths, Ruppert asked his wife if she'd mind joining him chez Max that morning, to help him with the phone calls he needed to make to the man's English relatives.

'Can you take some flexi-time off or something? Go in first thing and then come and join me?'

'I don't see why not. Me, acting as a translator – that sounds more interesting than my normal day. It's quiet at the moment. I don't think anyone will mind.'

With that she left and, a little later, acting on a hunch, Ruppert set off for the Hôtel Les Ateliers de l'Image, mindful that he had only a short time before he met up with Bonnet.

At the hotel, Ruppert showed the picture of Collins to the young man on the reception desk.

'I'm Commandant Ruppert and I'm investigating the

disappearance of this man, Clive Collins. I've got a few questions. Have you seen him and, if so, when? I'd also like you to check your records to tell me when you last had a Monsieur Sam Rodgers staying with you.'

'I think I'll have to get the manager, Commandant. He will be able to help you. I haven't seen the man in the photo, but I only started here last week. The manager is the one to ask. Please take a seat – there's a quiet area by the rear door along there,' he said, pointing to a short corridor off reception. 'Would you like a coffee?'

'No thanks. I'm in a rush. I'll come back if the manager isn't available straight away.'

Ruppert went to wait and, taking in the modern decor of the hotel with its large framed black and white prints of movie stars, found himself looking at the photographic and art books on the shelves in the little library he'd been sent to.

It was with some surprise that on one shelf, in a small selection of novels obviously left by guests for others to enjoy, he saw a copy of *Assassin* and picked it up. He'd just opened it to see it was a signed copy when the manager walked in.

'Commandant, how can we help you today?'

'I'm investigating a missing person . . . this man Clive Collins,' said Ruppert, showing him the photo. 'Have you seen him?'

'Oh, yes. He often comes in and has drinks in the old cinema or dines with us out on the terrace. He stays here in the tree-house room whenever his family come out to St Rémy because he can't stand the noise the grandchildren make.'

'When did you last see him?'

'Probably last month. I'd have to check the reservations for you to see when he last dined here. As to when he last used the bar, that might be problematical as sometimes he wouldn't be the one paying.'

'Who have you seen him with here?'

'All kinds of people, we like to think we run a discreet establishment for our guests.'

'Never mind all that, I'd like to know the names of any regular consorts of his.'

'There were, er, various women. I only recognised Madame Gardot from the art gallery in town and Lucille, the wife of Jacques Dersonne, the rock star. It's awkward for us because Jacques is a regular himself when he's in town and sometimes does the odd acoustic guitar session for us on our jazz evenings. I've told the staff that even if walls have ears, they must not speak, *ever*. That's what I mean about exercising discretion.'

'Have you ever seen him with Sam Rodgers, the author of this book, himself a regular guest of yours, I understand?'

'Yes, I did see them together from time to time, but I'd better tell you that the whole thing has to be carefully choreographed. Monsieur Rodgers wants to know if Monsieur Collins is booked in at the restaurant, in which case he'll eat elsewhere or take room service, and Collins wants to know if Rodgers is likely to be dining with us, in which case *he* won't book. It's ridiculous, because when they bump into each other from time to time, they seem friendly enough.'

'Has either of them ever said anything to you about the other?'

'No, which I find quite odd. I've never known the reason for the awkwardness. I thought maybe they'd fallen out over some woman or other.'

'When did you last see them together?'

'Last month. Monsieur Rodgers has been staying with us off and on.'

'Really? Do you remember *exactly* when you last saw them speaking to each other?'

'I don't, I'm afraid. I'm pretty sure I've seen them together in the last few weeks, but then again, I can't be sure. I'm sorry. I may not have seen them together for quite a while. I can't be certain.'

'When did Rodgers leave your hotel and why did you say his stay was "off and on"?'

'He left only a couple of days ago for the Château des Alpilles. He said it was quieter which would suit him better as he wanted to finish his latest book.'

'I'll need to know when he arrived last month, if you could find that out and call me on this number?'

Ruppert handed over his card. 'And, if he broke his stay with you, I'll need to know the dates he left and returned. Where did he go when he wasn't with you?'

'We made the bookings for him, a couple of short trips I think, from memory, a few days each time. He stayed at the Mas de la Fouque, a luxury hotel in the Camargue. An old girlfriend of mine runs the spa there. Let me know if you want to talk to her. She doesn't miss much, I can tell you, in my experience.'

'Now, Monsieur, as you've mentioned you can be discreet, let's put it to the test, shall we? You are not to tell Rodgers, if you see him, that I've been to talk to you. At all. Understand? Tell the receptionist the same, and anybody else on the staff who's seen me.'

*   *   *

Ruppert pondered this latest twist. Should he see Rodgers straight away and challenge him in a really tough interview, or, perhaps, would it be better to let him stew for a while and strike later? He was still cogitating that choice when he arrived at the Collins house to find Bonnet standing beside his car.

'Sorry, Bonnet. I've been to the Hôtel Les Ateliers de l'Image. Turns out Rodgers has been there off and on for a month and only moved to the des Alpilles a few days ago. So much for him telling us he'd just arrived.'

'I feel another interview coming on, sir.'

'Dead right, Bonnet.'

'Unfortunate turn of phrase, Commandant.'

'Yes, I suppose it was. It was a slip of the tongue, but we both think that Collins is missing, presumed dead, don't we?'

'It's looking that way, sir.'

'Trouble is, there's no shortage of suspects, only a dearth of bodies.'

Ruppert opened up the gates and they walked over to the house.

'What's the plan for today, boss?' asked Bonnet.

'I think I'd like you to go to Glanum and check out the CCTV for the tenth, the day Rachet says he took Collins there. Madame Ruppert is reading the Rodgers book and says his favoured method of disposing of people is in water. Check the shrine surrounding the sacred spring, there's water there … and the deep pond – the Nymphea – which is down some steps. The Romans used to perform religious rites there and that checks out with another of the obsessions in the book. Oh, and there may be some water by the Thermae section, I can't quite remember. I don't think you'll find anything, but you never know. We can always call up for a police diver if required, but check with me first.'

'So you think Rodgers could be our man?'

'I don't know. But let's say I'm forming a few thoughts

about his possible involvement. We've got a way to go yet, Lieutenant.'

As Bonnet walked back towards his car, Madame Ruppert passed him on her way in.

'I'm the new English interpreter,' she said to his raised eyebrows.

As he drove off watched by the Rupperts, she said to her husband, 'Well, I don't know what he made of me being your new translator. Where have you sent him?'

'Glanum, to look at the CCTV at the last place we know for certain that Collins went. I've also told him whilst he's there to look at some of the potential watery graves!'

'Maybe he thinks you've just got him out of the way.'

'Don't be ridiculous.'

*   *   *

Whilst Ruppert organised his phone and the names and phone numbers of the people he wanted to call, his wife had a snoop around. She called to him from the living room.

'Strange taste. It's like an English country house in part with some modern design thrown in. Eclectic and a bit kitsch. And what's that strange odour around the place?'

'Drains, I should think, and it's been shut up for a while. That sensitive nose of yours, really – I can't smell anything. Now, where are you? I'm ready when you are, chérie.'

Ruppert explained how they were going to do it.

'It'll be on speaker phone ... you should make it clear that you're the interpreter.'

'What do I say when they answer?'

'You'll know. Make it up as you go along.'

'Right, first up is the son, Stephen Baker. Don't say we think he might be dead, whatever you do ... OK!'

Ruppert phoned the number when he judged his wife was ready.

'Hello! Baker!' the son answered the call.

'Hello. Do you speak French?'

'No.'

'It's not a problem. It's the French police in St Rémy here and I am calling with Commandant Ruppert present. I am acting as interpreter for this conversation and you will hear the Commandant's voice from time to time speaking in French and I will translate.'

'What's happened? Any developments. I'm heartily sick at the lack of progress. Have you found my father?'

'Not yet. We are pursuing enquiries and making some progress. I understand from my colleagues that you are mystified by his disappearance. Can I ask you if you know of any enemies that your father had?'

'Enemies? Take your pick. Lovers, husbands, business associates he shafted. Look, I disapprove of him and his behaviour, that's why I took my mother's name. My wife and children like him because he flatters her and entertains them. I tolerate him because he is my father. What can you do? This is all a right nuisance.'

'But do you know anyone who would want to do him harm?'

'Wait a minute, are you saying he might have been murdered? I thought this was a missing person enquiry. What are you saying?'

'We are keeping an open mind and trying to investigate every possibility.'

'I don't know what to say. I don't know of anyone who would do that, no. Should I be worried? I mean what about paying his bills . . . is that down to me to sort out?'

'I didn't mean to alarm you. As for bills, we've seen recent bank statements and most regular payments are by direct debit. I'm sure Gérard can help with matters on the ground this end, but maybe his lawyers should be notified he's missing.'

'I'm going to speak to his solicitor here who handles his affairs in London and also does his French stuff through a notaire. He'll know what to do. I'll leave it all to him.'

'I didn't mean to panic you, Monsieur Baker. Can I ask if you intend to come out to St Rémy?'

'I run a restaurant. I can't just drop everything. I suppose if necessary I can and will come out, if I have to, but I'll need some notice. I'll speak to Gérard. What does he say about all this?'

'Gérard is being helpful. Rest assured, we are looking at every angle and as soon as we have any firm developments, we will let you know. Thank you, Monsieur Baker, and goodbye.'

'Goodbye. Keep me posted, please. I've got journalists calling all the time for updates and constantly mocking the "snail's pace" of the police in France.'

Ruppert ended the call and his wife translated the last part of the conversation.

'You were very good. You should do this for a living.'

'It was very stressful, but I loved it. What did you make of him? I was too busy trying to translate what he said and then concentrating on what you were trying to get me to say. I hope I did both of you justice.'

'It all sounded very smooth to me. Very impressive. As for Monsieur Baker, he seemed annoyed with all the bother it was causing him and he seemed, more or less, to be saying he'll only come for a funeral. That's nice.'

'Right, who's next? I'm really getting into this.'

'Wife number one. Fiona Baker.'

Soon the phone was ringing.

'Hello. Who's that?'

Madame Ruppert went through the same introductions and then asked, 'Do you have any information to offer about the disappearance of Monsieur Collins?'

There was a delay in the reply, so long that they thought they had lost the connection.

'. . . Sorry . . . it's just that I'm on my way to a meeting. I've always thought it was just a matter of time before things caught up with him. He is, you might as well know, in *my* opinion, an inveterate liar and a cheat. He can't help himself. He just isn't a decent human being. I'm not bitter, I'm really, really, not. I'm just speaking from my direct experience. Maybe things got too much for him and he grew as tired of himself as everybody else was. Is there any kind of suicide note? He'd want to have the last word. I'd look for that, if I were you. Look, I'm afraid I've got to go. Sorry I can't help you, goodbye.'

'Well she doesn't carry a torch for him, does she, Jules? I hope you wouldn't talk like that about me.'

'You can't take it personally,' Ruppert replied. 'She was quite restrained . . . '

'But completely uncaring about whether he was alive or dead,' his wife added.

'Yes, and, therefore, a disinterested party. We can rule her out.'

'Who's next. Another wife?'

'His second wife, Catriona Knight. Let's see if we can get three out of three. In the old days without mobiles, it could take days to get hold of people.'

Ruppert tapped the number into the mobile in front of them and his wife went into the same routine when it was answered. The reply to the question of, 'Do you have information about the disapperance of Clive Collins in France?' wasn't quite what either of them expected and they exchanged glances throughout the rather terse response from Madame Knight.

'I haven't got the foggiest idea of where he is or what's happened to him. You should try Mary Telford, she was his last English fling, as far as I know. Her husband still hasn't forgiven him for seducing his wife when they were out in St Rémy staying with him. That's what we're dealing with here, Inspector. A terrible flirt and serial womaniser who would swear all his friends to secrecy. He used to deny everything to me, of course, and said I was just a jealous cow whose green eyes could see into a parallel universe where he slept with anyone and everyone. Well, it turned out he had. No loyalty. There has to be a basic level of trust for any marriage to survive. Deceit was his middle name. He just wasn't on my side, ever . . . Hello . . . are you still there?'

'Yes, Madame, just a moment, I will check what further questions we have.'

'When did you last see Monsieur Collins?'

'That's easy. Fifteen years ago when we had a meeting with our solicitors to finalise the financial arrangements of our divorce. Is that all?'

'Yes, thank you, Madame.'

They both looked at each other.

'You know. It makes us look blissfully happy, Jules,

doesn't it.'

'Yes. What a carry on. Most of the criminals I come into contact with have a more advanced moral code than Monsieur Max has.'

'Any more people to call? What about this Mary Telford? Her husband might want revenge, do you think?'

'Maybe. I'll see if I can find a number here in these papers and address book.'

'Whilst you do that, I'll make us a coffee. I can see a jar of that instant stuff only the Brits seem to buy at Intermarché. Do you know they've got a special shelf of English products now? What happened to "when in Rome"?'

Ruppert finally found the number just as his wife was opening the fridge to look for some milk.

'The fridge is empty, nothing at all. I didn't expect that, did you?'

'I think Gérard must have emptied it. Why do you ask?'

'Would he have done that when he didn't know then that his boss wasn't going to return? I mean, butter and things last a while.'

'That is odd. I'll have to ask him. He's sure to come up with something plausible though.'

She brought over the black coffees.

'Here we are,' Ruppert said, ' here's the number. Our final call, with any luck.'

The same process elicited a startled response from Mary Telford who had not, until then, heard that Clive Collins had disappeared. She was tearful at first when told the news, but recovered to say, 'That must explain why I haven't heard from him. He'd told me it was all over, but I kept hoping it wasn't true. I forced myself not to bother him, hoping that he'd come round in the end and see sense.'

'Can you tell us if your husband had continued contact with Monsieur Collins?'

'Roger? Hardly. He said he would never speak to him again. They were best friends, you know.'

'Was he very angry when he found out and did he bear a grudge against Monsieur Collins?'

'Roger? He knew what Clive was like and accepted him for who he was, never saying anything when it was other people's wives he went off with. We separated and Roger went off to take a job in Singapore and has been there ever since. Too embarrassed, he said, to be in the same country as all of his old friends. He couldn't bear the shame of it. You can imagine how that made me feel. That's why I clung on to the hope that Clive and I would end up together as that would at least make some sense of it.'

'What do you think has happened to Monsieur Collins?'

'I'm hoping he's gone to a retreat to try and sort himself out, for my sake. He sometimes said he dreamt about taking himself off for a proper spiritual cleanse.'

'Did he mention any names of likely places?'

'The only one he mentioned was one that he said he'd never go back to because he'd lapsed, had an affair with the yoga teacher and got thrown out.'

'Well, thank you, Madame.'

'You will let me know what happens? If you don't, nobody else will.'

'Yes, of course, and you can call us on this number if you've not heard from us in a week or so.'

Ruppert turned to his wife.

'Actually a good hit rate. Four out of four. That's it, for now. How do you feel?'

'Exhausted, but exhilarated. Rather saddened by that last call. She was tragic, wasn't she?'

'Lost everything on one throw of the dice, by the sound of it. My opinion of Monsieur Max is lower than ever, but I can't help feeling, they would all say that, wouldn't they?'

'Jules. It's more than that. The man obviously can only relate to women by bedding them. Then he discards them. No understanding at all. What a shallow man, just hell-bent on the next fling like a junkie after a fix. He must have needed the aphrodisiac of constant conquests to bolster a low self-esteem. That's what I think, for what it's worth.'

'Wow. Psychological insights as well as fluency in English. I'm lucky you stay with me.'

'Jules, my dear, it's not like that and anyway, who can be bothered to have affairs?'

'Monsieur Max proves that to us, but clearly he thought he was having a whale of a time.'

'Is that me finished now? Can I go back to the town

hall? It'll seem very tame and boring after this.'

'What are you going to do about lunch?'

'I'll get something on my way and work through lunch today, I think. Will you be OK?'

'Yes, I can fend for myself, thanks.'

Madame Ruppert gave him a kiss and left.

∗   ∗   ∗

Ruppert called Bonnet to find out how he was getting on.

'They took ages to find the tapes for the tenth and then the machine wouldn't work. I've just started looking at them now, so I've got a couple of hours still to go here, I think, including looking at the water features as requested. How did the new interpreter work out?'

'My wife was excellent, thanks. She is fluent in English and has a degree in it.'

'I hope you don't mind me saying it, sir, but shouldn't you have used one of our official translators?'

'By the time you've fixed up for the travel here and briefed them, it would be the middle of next week. Anyway, these were only informal conversations. I'd go official if we needed to go the formal interview route. As it turns out, I think it was a waste of time, other than casting a light on the loose morals of Monsieur Max. I'll make some notes and you can read those. What'll you do for lunch?'

'I'll grab something from the café here and press on. What about you?'

'I'm going to see the neighbours and then I'll go into town and perhaps see if Madame Gardot is at her gallery. Phone me when you've finished.'

No sooner had he put the phone down on Bonnet, than the manager of the Hôtel Les Ateliers de l'Image phoned to give him the dates Rodgers stayed and when he'd broken his stay to go to the Camargue – one of those dates being the ninth of the previous month, and when he'd left for the Château des Alpilles. He also gave him the name of his old girlfriend at the Mas de La Fouque.

*   *   *

Now, Ruppert felt ready to tackle the neighbours, for what it was worth. Trying to banish negative thoughts, he strode purposefully next door and rang the bell for Monsieur and Madame Sim. He soon found an elderly couple standing at their front door – Monsieur, incongruously dressed in a pair of Speedos and Madame in a housecoat with her hair in curlers, both of them looking relaxed and quite ready for him as if they'd dressed up for the occasion. Perhaps they had, he thought.

They invited him into a very gloomy dining room, full of dark furniture, which surprised him given that the house was a new-build in the Provençal style.

Straight away Madame was off, leaving her husband only to nod in agreement at certain points.

'The comings and goings, Monsieur. We told the Lieutenant, we've always wondered what goes on in there. Different women, drinks parties and he's never invited us. Not that we would go. He's not interested in us. Too grand. We tried to sell him the garage that adjoins his property and ours. We gave him a price and all he could say was, "For you ... very reasonable, for me ... too dear." Every time we dropped the price, he said the same thing, until the price got so low we'd have been giving it away. And he never listened to a word I said. I saw him once in town and I told him my mother had died. And do you know what he said? He said, "Very good." Can you believe it? He thinks he's too clever by half that one, doesn't he?'

Her husband nodded.

'Tell me, Madame and Monsieur,' said Ruppert, 'have you seen anything over the past month that might help me in my search for your neighbour?'

They looked at each other, shaking their heads.

'No, Monsieur,' they said in unison, before she added, 'What'll happen to the house if he doesn't come back?'

Ruppert said he didn't know and thanked them for their time. He left and walked back round to the main road. He had to ring on the bell by the front gate where there was still a brass plate for Doctor Antoine du Perry. Ruppert thought that was slightly odd as he knew the good Doctor had been dead for quite a few years. Maybe his widow couldn't quite bring herself to remove it, or perhaps she thought her status would suffer if she did.

He was soon buzzed in and found himself looking at a very elegant woman, probably in her late sixties – very much a doppelganger for the actress Stéphane Audran – who was clearly no stranger to the hairdressers, beauty salons and elegant clothes shops of St Rémy.

He wasn't going to be invited in, that was plain, but, with her rather forbidding expression, he thought that was probably just as well.

He'd already introduced himself at the entry-phone at the gate, so Ruppert felt able to start his questions, more or less without any preamble.

'I'll come straight to the point, Madame. Have you seen anything in the past month that could help us with our enquiries about your neighbour?'

'I see very little of him. I rarely look out of the rear windows and, when I do, I always seem to see that dreadful little man Sim scuttling about in his garden in those disgusting swimming trunks of his.' She shuddered. 'Monsieur Collins hardly spoke to me and that was made worse when I objected to his plans to build a swimming pool. As you can see, I lost that argument.'

'No unusual noises or anything like that?'

'I'm either listening to the radio or watching the television in the evening, so I don't hear a thing from the outside, not even those dreadful piping frogs that infest the irrigation channels that run everywhere around here.'

'You don't like Monsieur Collins, I take it?'

'We've always had a very formal relationship, apart from the first time we met. He came around here when he moved in and seemed to be very enthusiastic about inviting me to come in for drinks. Of course I refused, not least because of what the neighbours would say, but it was more than that. Straight away, I could tell he was the sort of the man who thinks that persistence gets you everywhere with women and with some, it's true, that's all it does take. Not with me. I simply told him that it would never happen. He didn't ask me again and could barely acknowledge me if we passed in the street. The swimming pool saga even put paid to that basic level of intimacy.'

'Thank you, Madame, that's been, er, very illuminating.' He turned to leave.

'I understand irony, Commandant. But . . . wait . . . I have remembered something. Of late, there has been the smell of diesel on a few occasions, just like I used to get from that dreadful plumber's van when the swimming pool was being installed.'

Ruppert had turned to listen to this final piece of information and wasn't at all sure what to make of it.

'Thank you, Madame. I don't think I'll have to bother you again.'

He almost went to tip his hat to her, until he remembered he wasn't wearing one. Monsieur Max was certainly up for a challenge, he thought.

*   *   *

Back at the house, Ruppert shuffled through some of the post that Gérard had obviously opened and put on the desk in the study. He wondered if Collins was happy about Gérard doing that, or whether it was something new that the guardian had taken it upon himself to do. To give him the benefit of the doubt, perhaps he'd started doing it after speaking to Collins' son. Those thoughts reminded Ruppert to check the post box at the front gate as Gérard wasn't there to do it every day. Looking around for the key, he found a likely looking one in the pencil tray.

He retrieved the post and noticed a bank statement covering the past month. Feeling it was within his rights, he opened it. A large withdrawal of fifteen thousand euros on the ninth caught his eye. That's a large sum for a mainly cheque man, he thought, and cashed the day before he went to Glanum.

There were no other cash withdrawals or card and cheque payments after that, only regular direct debits. Strange that uniform didn't seem to have examined recent bank transactions. No, not strange, it was slipshod, even if they had jumped to the conclusion, as others had, that Collins was just staying with some woman and would turn up again, bright-eyed and bushy-tailed.

He was annoyed with himself and thumped the table. He knew that's how mistakes happen. He should have spotted the error earlier instead of taking it for granted that colleagues had actually done what was expected of them.

Assuming other people have done their job properly is no excuse for you not doing yours, thought Ruppert. Having the information now, early in his own investigation, was little comfort to him.

He'd had enough at the house for one morning, and he strolled into town after locking up. Before going to Brasserie du Commerce in Place de la République for a spot of lunch, he thought he'd try and catch Madame Gardot at her eponymous gallery just down the road on Boulevard Marceau. He was in luck, she was there, but just about to close. She recognised him and let him in.

'Hello, Commandant. I wondered when I might have the honour of a visit. I understand you are looking into Max's disappearance.'

Entering the very upmarket gallery for the first time in his life, Ruppert was struck by how out of place he felt surrounded by modern art and sculpture. No wonder he'd never set foot in there before. Maybe for Monsieur Max, the main attraction of doing so was the heavily made-up Madame Gardot, in close-up a magnificent work of art herself. To be fair, putting himself in Monsieur Max's shoes, as he was beginning – rather alarmingly – to do, he could see that she was a temptation. She was yet another attractive woman of a certain age.

'I understand you know Monsieur Collins well, Madame.'

'He's bought a lot of art works from me. I'm sure you will have seen the series of oil paintings of sunflowers at his home. Those were all from here, although he is rather old-fashioned in his taste.'

'When did you last see him?'

'Early last month, he rang to ask me out for lunch, but I couldn't go, which was a pity as I could usually sell him something and he's always tried to support my business. I looked out for him at that week's market, but he wasn't there. I assumed he was out of town on one of his trips.'

'Where did you think he had gone?'

'It could have been to any number of places. England, Paris, the Camargue. Until I read that he'd gone missing I had thought no more about it. Now, I'm worried.'

'Did he ever talk about problems with people? With people who might do him harm?'

'No. I knew he sailed close to the wind, as far as women and their husbands were concerned, but he never expressed any fears for his safety. Are you telling me he might have been killed?'

'No, I'm not saying that. I'm just making enquiries at this stage.'

'If I knew where he might be or who might have done him harm, I would tell you, Commandant.'

'Tell me about your own position, Madame. Exactly how close *are* you to Monsieur Collins?'

'Ah, I see. I know your wife saw me having lunch with him once. What did she say?'

'That has nothing to do with it. I'm trying to establish your relationship with Collins, that's all.'

'I'm a married woman. Monsieur Collins is a good customer. I've always tried to give him what he wanted, apart from that one thing – my art was up against the wall, I wasn't.'

'Did your husband ever think that there was more to your association with Collins than dealer and client?'

'Did *he* kill him? If you mean that, why not ask it?'

'*If* Collins has been murdered, naturally we will look at whether it was a *crime passionnel* and that means we would be connecting relevant women to Collins and seeing who else linked to them might be involved.'

'*Cherchez la femme*! How exciting!'

'I'll ask again. Your husband . . . ?'

'My husband is a notaire. He knows he can trust me, just as I trust him. Monsieur Collins is a player. He likes the chase. I like being chased, but I don't get caught. I wouldn't risk everything for a man like him.'

'Do you have any idea of what might have happened to him?'

'You could be on the right lines. He's tried it on with most of the women who own shops in St Rémy, but they all joke that, like President Chirac, he's probably another Mr Three Minutes, shower included. Yvette at Le Saigon knows him better than the rest of us. You could try her. She might have more insight than I do. You're barking up the wrong tree with me, Commandant. Sorry.'

Ruppert sat in the Bar du Commerce and enjoyed his croque monsieur served with a green salad and washed down with a glass of Domaine de Valdition rosé. Something he could rely on at last – served on a plate and viewed through a glass.

He felt he was getting nowhere. He'd give anything to be working on some organised crime where the villains were obvious and straightforward. With them, what you see is what you get. The past few days had been spent looking at the so-called elite. He wasn't sure which set of people was worse than the other.

He took two phone calls on the way back to the Collins house. The first was from Bonnet saying he was on his way back from Glanum – he'd found the footage of Collins, but there was no sign of him having met anyone else there that day and he was certain there wasn't a body in any of the pools. It turned out that some of the tapes from the tenth had already been recorded over and there was a lot of footage missing, unfortunately. So much for that line of enquiry.

The second call was from his wife who said she was calling from outside the office because she wanted to tell him that Christian Taval had seemed to be very interested in knowing how the Commandant's enquiries were progressing. Naturally, she said, she'd told him nothing.

Ruppert told her he might be late that evening as he'd decided over his lunch to head off to the Camargue to follow up his enquiries. He'd either eat out or pick at some leftover cheese when he returned home and she shouldn't wait for him.

Bonnet turned the corner into Chemin de Figuières Folles pretty much as Ruppert arrived, so they both reached the house together and Bonnet lowered his car window.

'Don't get out, Lieutenant. We're off on a jaunt to the Camargue, if that's OK with you.'

'Jump in, sir. It's fine by me.'

As Ruppert strapped himself in, Bonnet asked, 'Where to, boss?'

'Mas de la Fouque in Saintes Maries de la Mer. Do you know it? It's on the Route de Petit Rhône a few miles out of town.'

'Know it, sir. It's where I spent the first night after my wedding. We could only afford one night, but we had a blast, let me tell you.'

'Maybe not, Bonnet. Spare me the details, please.'

'Is this where our man Rodgers stayed?'

'That's right. It's going to be useful that you know your way around.'

6.

Driving out of St Rémy and then up the Avenue Vincent Van Gogh, they passed, on the right, the Roman Triumphal Arch and, on the left, first the St Paul de Mausole clinic – where the artist Van Gogh had been treated – and then, immediately, the entrance to Glanum, before heading over the Alpilles through the winding pass.

Soon they were on the other side, driving downhill past the vineyards of Mas de la Dame and others on the southern slopes. This way, via Maussane and Paradou, was Ruppert's preferred way to the Camargue.

Driving along the straight roads of the plain, they passed field after field of sunflowers. Skirting around the eastern flank of Arles, and passing the long low Roman aqueduct, they briefly joined the motorway to Nîmes. Crossing the mighty Rhône, they took the road off to Saintes Maries de la Mer.

That put them almost immediately into the Camargue

and the coast road through its vast fields of growing rice. Passing them, Ruppert then enjoyed spotting the white horses, the bulls, the flamingos and the *gardiens'* white houses with their ridged, thatched roofs.

On the way, he had filled Bonnet in with the results of his morning's interviews and also his theories about the case based on what they knew so far. But he knew that they were, at best, merely speculation. He was losing his touch, he knew it. Bonnet had pressed him on who he thought had 'actually bumped Monsieur Max off' and he'd had to admit he didn't really know.

He'd fallen into silence by the time they drove through Saintes Maries, the town on the coast that made you think you were in Spain with its almost uniformly low white houses sprawled astride the main road through it.

The Mas de la Fouque itself was like an adobe hacienda, more California than Provence, set by its very own étang.

Walking into the all-white reception, with its high, vaulted and whitewashed wooden ceiling, Ruppert could see the appeal of the place to a man like Rodgers.

The receptionist was helpful, confirming that Rodgers was a regular guest, even adding that he would write for hours sitting in the jacuzzi and sipping champagne. After confirming that Rodgers had stayed from the ninth to the fifteenth and then from the twentieth to the twenty-seventh, he rang the spa for them and asked the manager to come through as she had visitors, before generously ordering them coffees. Soon they were joined at a table outside by Madeline, Ruppert's contact, who'd been told by the manager of the Hôtel Les Ateliers de l'Image to expect a visit from him.

'So, Madeline. Did you get to know Monsieur Rodgers well?'

'Only in the sense that he would come here quite often. To write, he said, but I saw little evidence of that.'

'Maybe, like Georges Simenon, he was up at dawn to write for five hours before breakfast,' Ruppert said.

'With the hangovers Monsieur Rodgers usually has, I doubt that,' replied Madeline.

'When he was here, did he used to meet anybody?'

'From time to time, yes. He would be joined for lunch. It was always men, I noticed, but I never knew who they were. Recently he saw the same two men on two occasions.'

'What did they look like?'

'Dark-haired like the local cowboys but, by the way they dressed and behaved, they couldn't have been.'

'Did you ever see this man?' Ruppert asked, showing Madeline the photo of Collins.

'Not with Rodgers, although he came to stay here last year. Why?'

'He's missing.'

'I can't remember his name. Who is he?'

'Clive Collins – also known as Monsieur Max.'

'Monsieur Max? I think I heard Rodgers talking about

him one day. Maybe it was on the phone, or with those other men. "Monsieur Max," he said in a loud voice, I'm sure of it.'

'And you're sure that this man, Max, hasn't been here in the last month?'

'Not when I've been on duty, but I do have days off, and I had nearly a week off last month, Commandant.'

'But tell me, did Rodgers ever leave the place during his stay?'

'Recently, he did come and go quite a lot, either off for the day, or every few days he'd pack and leave. He said he had to return to St Rémy.'

'What's your opinion of Monsieur Rodgers?'

'I don't really like to say.'

'You can say anything you like to me, Madeline. It won't go any further.'

'Creepy. He has two massages a day, our caviar body treatment in the morning and our de-ageing treatment in the late afternoon.'

'Isn't that normal at a spa hotel?'

'Not really. And not twice a day. And not when you ask, "Any extras today, Madamoiselle?" every single time.'

'Well, thanks, Madeline.'

'You should come and stay, Monsieur, and bring your wife.'

'The Lieutenant has stayed, haven't you, Bonnet?'

'Yes and we loved it. The bedrooms are amazing and just look at the place. Madeline's right, sir, you should treat Madame Ruppert.'

'Maybe. One day, perhaps.'

They thanked Madeline again, and then had a walk around the grounds.

'Plenty of water here, boss. We could keep the frogmen busy for weeks.'

'Who do you think the two men Rodgers was seeing were?'

'Could be anyone. Sounded like she thought they were from the Camargue. Local colour for his latest novel? But, it was strange she thought they were talking about Collins.'

'Where to now, sir?'

'Let's head back. We can call in at Club Paradis Plage. Collins kept its card by his phone. We passed it on the way here. See what they can tell us, if anything, about the missing Monsieur Max.'

*   *   *

They were admitted with some reluctance to Club Paradis Plage. It was a wooden shack, on raised decking, fenced off from the beach and reached by walking across the burning sand on a wooden boardwalk. The patron was a dark-haired local cowboy, as Madeline would have described him, thought Ruppert. He had been pointed out to them by the greeter, but it turned out that when they walked over to make themselves known to him, Eduardo, as he introduced himself, said he was sorry, but with Bonnet in uniform, it would look like he was being raided and he wasn't happy for them to be there.

This annoyed Ruppert.

'Sounds to me, Monsieur, like you've something to hide? Drugs? Do you want me to come back with a warrant?'

'No, sorry, you misunderstand me. On my life, I swear this is a clean place. It's just that my clients come here to relax and not to worry. A uniform disturbs that.'

'We make the world safe for your clients. How do you think we do that? Sorry we can't do it invisibly. And who are your clients? Do *they* have something to hide? How about Lieutenant Bonnet here goes round and takes their names and addresses.'

'What? Please, Monsieur. I beg you. The only wrong-doing he'll find is the odd person who's with someone they shouldn't be. That's all. I'm sorry, Monsieur. Sit down over here with me, and let's have a drink. On the house. Anything you want.'

'Some water would be nice.'

Water was ordered and briefly they glanced down over the rows of sunbathers flaked out below the decked terrace and let their eyes take in the gentle lapping waters of the Med.

'Do you know this man?' Ruppert asked, almost tired of asking and showing the photo of Collins to people who couldn't help him.

Eduardo laughed.

'Why, it's Monsieur Max. Every time he rings us up, he says the same thing. Every time. Every year. We know it's him from his very first words. He says in very stilted, old-fashioned French, "Good day. I would like to make a reservation for lunch for two people and to reserve two sailors." "Ah, Monsieur Max," we say, and he's always surprised that we know who it is. We've never told him that he gets the word for "lounger" mixed up with the word for "sailor"!'

'When did you last see him? I'm only interested in the last month.'

'I'll have to check the reservations book, Commandant. Hang on a sec whilst I fetch it.'

Bonnet was casting an eye over the flesh on display and Ruppert allowed him his moment. Eduardo returned with a large, well-used diary and turned the pages.

'Ah, here it is. The last entry is for a lunchtime booking on the eleventh for two people.'

'Do you remember who he was with?'

'I haven't been in this business for this long without noticing things. He usually comes with a woman, not always the same one, but that's his affair. Eduardo takes it all in. But this time, I was surprised. He was with a man who told me he was staying at the Mas de la Fouque. I think he was trying to impress on me that he was a man of means.'

'Anything else you can remember?'

'They had a heated discussion at one point and the Fouque guy had drunk most of a bottle of rosé by then, but the noise level was quite high in here so it didn't matter. That man left abruptly and, over his coffee and paying the bill, Monsieur Max said to me, "Eduardo, I envy you this life," which surprised me. He clearly doesn't know how much hard work it is, but I asked him what made him say that. Do you know what he told me? He said, "I think I might have made a bit of a mess of things. Unfortunately, Eduardo, I can't undo it all now." He left me a twenty euro tip and said he was off back to St Rémy.'

'Anything else strike you about him that day?'

'No. It was the first time he hadn't been acting the rich socialite he usually did.'

'Well, thank you, Eduardo,' said Ruppert. 'That's been very helpful. I appreciate it. We'll leave you now and you can reassure any anxious customers that we'd called in for a friendly chat. If you like, you can also tell them that we'll eventually catch up with them another day.'

Eduardo laughed and shook hands with Ruppert and Bonnet, walking them over to the exit as he did so, and then he stood waving at them as if to make sure they were actually going.

Out of sight and earshot and heading back to the car,

Bonnet turned to Ruppert.

'Eduardo's a bit of a rogue, isn't he?'

'Yes. More than a bit, I suspect, and rude with it. Did you notice that he only takes cash? I wonder if the tax people might care to investigate him? What did you make of what he said?'

'About Collins being depressed? Maybe it *was* suicide after all.'

'A moment of reflection, perhaps, but Collins wouldn't want that as the final act. He was more showbiz than that. And, we'd have found the body by now in all likelihood. The fact that we haven't done so points, in my experience, to something more sinister.'

'What if he'd hurled himself from the battlements of Les Baux, or drowned himself somewhere remote in the Camargue, the body might not be found for some considerable time.'

'From what we've established, Bonnet, wouldn't you say, knowing him as we do, that there would have been a suicide note to make it more of a dramatic exit?'

'Yes. Damn it. I suppose you're right. Back to the drawing board.'

'Well, Lieutenant, we're getting closer on the dates now. We know Collins was here on the eleventh. So Glanum was a red herring perhaps. The question is, what happened after he left here?'

*　　*　　*

Ruppert was feeling a bit more positive. Was the investigation turning? And in his favour?

As they headed back through the Camargue, he thought they should do a case review.

'At this point in any enquiry, Bonnet, I try and put a bit of pressure on the key players. Who do you think they are?'

'I still think the husbands are the best bet. Monsieur Max was going around and making them all look like fools. That's got to hurt, a lot. It may even drive a man to go a bit crazy. You've got to say that old Max was playing with fire, wasn't he, and was bound to get burnt somewhere along the line. So my top candidates would be: Melanie's builder bloke, maybe even rock star Jacques, oh, and I'll throw in Taval, because he's well dodgy. So I'd round them all up and give them the third degree.'

'Fair comments, Lieutenant, but whilst I agree that we should probably see Jacques Dersonne, I am not sure this is one of those crimes. I think we both agree that Collins has met a sticky end but I'm not sure jealous husbands are our answer.'

'Who's on your list then, sir?'

'I kind of agree about Taval, but I'm not convinced. I'm keeping Rodgers in the reckoning as I can't help thinking he's involved in some way although I'm still not sure how.'

'I bet Madame Ruppert already knows whodunnit, boss. Wives usually know best.'

'You're right there. I can't get away with anything at home. Maybe those are the skills we need in a case like this.'

Driving back the way they'd come, Ruppert asked Bonnet if he'd mind pulling into Château d'Estoublon, near Fontvieille, on the Route de Maussane.

'I want to buy some of their wine and olive oil. Perhaps I can bribe my wife to lend some of her intuition to solving the mystery of the missing Monsieur Max.'

As they pulled into the car park and Bonnet parked in the shade, Ruppert got out of the car.

'I'll only be a few minutes. See if you can find the number for Lucille Lamb. Let's try and see her husband and put your theories to the test. He might even be able to see us on our way.'

Ruppert was soon back in the car with his purchases and ready to phone to fix to meet Jacques Dersonne, which was, fortunately, easily arranged.

A fairly short drive later and they were once again at the elegant *mas* with its glorious views of Les Baux.

Lucille greeted them and explained that Jacques was in his studio at the back of the house and expecting them.

'Jacques wanted you to go to the studio. I told him you'd already spoken to me and would probably want to see him on his own. He's fine about it. You can take this path, which will lead you to the stone and glass barn. That's where you'll find him. And please, Commandant, please, please, please remember that I'd like my marriage to last.'

*   *   *

Jacques Dersonne was every inch a rock star. Maybe his hair was too long and his jeans too tight. Perhaps he'd seen better days, but the present day seemed pretty good to Ruppert. Bonnet was overawed and it showed.

'Come in,' said Jacques who had seen them through the wall of glass that made up one whole side of the barn. As they walked up, he'd opened the bifold doors to welcome them. Seeing Bonnet almost bowing to him, he tried to put him at his ease.

'Fifi,' he called into the dark interior of the studio, 'these are the police on a drugs raid. Hide all the gear.' He turned to Bonnet. 'Just joking. Seriously, go through,' he gestured to Bonnet. 'I've asked Fifi to make us some tea. You can have a look around and feel free to pick up a signed CD if you're interested.'

Ruppert shook his head to Bonnet and, already, felt the interview slipping away from him. Well, go with the flow, he thought. See where it takes me.

'Thank you for seeing us, Monsieur,' he said.

'You can't call a musician "Monsieur", Monsieur!' Jacques replied. 'Anyway, I take it this is an informal chat. That's what Lucille said it was going to be. By the way, did you know that BB King called his favourite guitar "Lucille"? I bet she's less highly strung than *my* Lucille.'

'I'm sorry to intrude on your work, but there are a few questions I have about Clive Collins, the man who has disappeared. I'm sure your wife will have told you.'

'Yes, she did. Did she tell you I don't care for him at all?'

'So I gather, but still, I assume you wouldn't have wanted him to disappear?'

'Well, I wouldn't care one way or another, but I, personally, wouldn't have done anything to make it happen.'

'When did you last see him?'

'No idea. Lucille knows to keep our paths uncrossed, if you know what I mean. Look, I'm aware he has a thing about actresses and that he and Lucille used to be an item, but I also know that he's too flighty to be a threat. He said to me once that he "smoked women" and was a "fifty-a-year man". "I'm an addict, Jacques," he said, "with a habit I can't kick." Then he smiled and delivered the punchline. "Guess what, I'm addicted to knickertine!" The guy was just a jerk and a sleazeball. I think he thought he was talking to a "rock musician" stereotype, with groupies, one-night stands and touring orgies, but that's just not me. I've never met anyone so keen on celebrity as him, sucking up to it, name dropping, trying to get into bed with anyone remotely famous and he's kept that going even at his age. Christ man, he's as old as I am.'

'Is the fact that your wife still sees him not troubling to you at all?'

'You mean, does it bother me? No is the answer. And I realised some time ago that Lucille is somehow like him. She's always been the same. Let me be really honest with you. I don't care. Why? Because I've got Monique in Paris. I don't give a damn what happens down here when I'm not around. Lucille knows how to run this place and we get on well enough. If it ain't broke, why fix it?'

'You seem very relaxed about it all. Can you tell me where you were the first couple of weeks of last month?'

'Fifi? Fifi? Bring the diary through will you?' As his assistant came over, trailing Bonnet, Jacques asked her to hand the diary to the 'nice Monsieur'.

Ruppert looked at the diary. The first two weeks of last month were scored out – PARIS.

'Seems you were in Paris. Did you return to Provence during that time?'

'No. And Monique can vouch for that. Lucille was here all that time though,' Jacques said pointedly. 'I hope you find Max alive, I really do, but I'd be lying if I said I care one way or the other. By the way,' he added, 'Lucille doesn't know about Monique. Can we keep it that way, if you don't mind?'

Ruppert nodded and, shaking hands with Jacques Dersonne, he and Bonnet thanked him and Fifi and left.

Lucille was waiting for them by the car.

'How was that, Commandant?'

'Interesting, shall we say, Madame, but don't worry he didn't learn any more from us than we learnt from him, except maybe we now know that you're like a finely tuned guitar.'

'Oh! That's nice. Is that it with us both now, as far as you're concerned? What next in the hunt for Collins? You think he's dead, don't you?'

'The next few days will turn out to be crucial in us finding out what's happened to the missing Monsieur Max, Madame, and we'll keep you informed.'

Ruppert and Bonnet drove back to St Rémy slightly shell-shocked.

'Nobody has a good word about Collins do they, sir? I'm beginning to feel sorry for the man. I heard most of what Jacques Dersonne said and Fifi kept saying to me that he "hates that man, hates him". I wonder if it was an act. I wouldn't be at all surprised if he'd paid a hit man to get rid of him.'

'I think Jacques is too busy trying to chase other hits, Bonnet, than to bother with Collins. I got the impression he quite likes to think that, if his wife is squired, I think that's the right word, by someone as shallow as Collins, he can happily get on with living his own life. I think Jacques Dersonne is off my list.'

'In that case, sir, it wasn't a wasted trip. What about that studio set-up. Terrific. You're right. Why risk all that for someone like Collins, especially as it turns out that Monsieur Dersonne is basically the same sort of man, despite what he says. It takes one to know one, sir.'

'I thought for a moment our rock star was going to be different. Idols are human, Bonnet, with the same faults as the rest of us. Disappointing, isn't it?'

'Where does it leave us?'

'I want to see the last of the women that we haven't yet interviewed, Yvette Brulls at Le Saigon. I think I'll ring her now. She should be at work.'

Having found a number for the restaurant, Ruppert was soon speaking to her.

'Hello, Madame Brulls? I'm Commandant Ruppert and I'm investigating the disappearance of Monsieur Clive Collins. When can I come and see you for a chat?'

'I'm busy preparing for the evening's service, so now is not a good time. If you come at nine o'clock tonight, all the mains will be away and I can leave my sous chef to finish off. Maybe we could have a dessert or a digestif on the terrace then, if it's not too late for you.'

Ruppert agreed to the time and said to Bonnet that he didn't need him to give up his evening as well. It was a short stroll to the Boulevard Mirabeau for Ruppert from his house and he thought it would be better to do the interview on his own. By then they were back in St Rémy.

'You can drop me off by the church, Bonnet, and call

it a night. I can handle Yvette Brulls,' he said to the Lieu-tenant, who grinned and replied, 'I'm sure you can, sir.'

Smiling at that, Ruppert got out of the car and asked Bonnet to meet him at the Collins house at the usual time in the morning.

*   *   *

Ruppert and his wife decided when they met up at home to go out for a crepe at Lou Planet. They sat outside in Place Favier, looking at the children playing by the little square's fountain on the warm evening, and they brought themselves up to date with their day.

Madame Ruppert had more to say about Christian Taval. She, without him knowing, had looked at other files on the Collins house and discovered that Rodgers had also had run-ins with the town council's planning department. It seems that anything an expat wanted to do was given extra-special scrutiny. The same architect was involved both times as well as the same planning officer, Christian Taval.

'So, what are you suggesting?' he asked.

'I think you should see the architect, Jules, don't you?'

'Very well. You never know. What's his name?'

'Emmanuel Loisel. He has that smart little office on Boulevard Gambetta, by the florist's.'

'I know it. I'll see him tomorrow. Now, do you want a dessert? There may be time before I have to go for mine at Le Saigon.'

'No thanks, you go. I'll sit here and watch the world over a cup of coffee and pay the bill. See you later.'

With that Ruppert got up, kissed his wife on the cheek and left.

He walked past the Nostradamus wall fountain on Rue Carnot and couldn't resist tossing some cents into its trough, hoping a little clairvoyance might result.

In a few moments, he was seated with the owner at a table on the small raised terrace outside Le Saigon, an elegant little Vietnamese restaurant. Yvette Brulls, the chef/patron, ordered a plate of banh tieu and moon cake with jasmine tea for both of them, which was served and eaten as they talked.

'Are you sure you don't want a digestif, Monsieur?'

'Quite sure, thanks, but don't let me stop you.'

'I rarely drink, but I might have a Gauloise at some point. Now, how can I help you in your quest for the elusive Monsieur Max?'

'I'm told you're good friends. Is that so?'

'It's true. "My very own Miss Saigon" he calls me, but I've never seen the show, so it's wasted on me. He stayed late drinking cognac here, years ago, and one thing led to another. If he books himself in – usually on a Saturday because I don't open Sundays – I know how the night will end. You might not think too highly of me because of that, Commandant, but you see, he's like me, a bit of a loner. Ships that pass in the night, that's what we are and, from time to time, that's a comfort to both of us. I'm sure you don't approve, do you?'

'I'm not here to judge, Madame, only to investigate a man's disappearance. Any light you can shed on that would be appreciated.'

'I'm trying to say that I only see him from time to time. I know what he is and that he's using me, but ... I'm using him too. I'm not sure he knows that. He's very vain, you know, and thinks he's God's gift to women. I haven't had the heart to tell him he isn't. I want to explain. You see, my father started this restaurant. He'd been in the catering corps with the French army in Indo-China after the war and, when he retired, he opened this place and brought over Vietnamese chefs. I worked on the tables when I came back from university and any stray men dining here thought it was fun to flirt and try and get off with me. A lot succeeded. It was fun, but when my father died, I took over the whole place, the cooking as well because I'd worked a lot in the kitchen too by then, and it became all-consuming, the cooking, running the restaurant, the casual flings. And look, I'm in my sixties and I'm still doing it all.'

'When did you last see Monsieur Max?'

'I'm not sure. I can check. Most times he makes a

reservation.'

She went to fetch the book and returned with it open.

'He was booked in on the thirteenth of last month, a Saturday, but the thing is, I've no recollection of whether he came or not because there's no tick by his name. That's our system but it hasn't worked this time.'

'This is quite important, Madame. Can you try and think carefully?'

She lit a cigarette – as if it would aid the process of remembering the last night she'd seen Collins.

'I just can't. Sometimes he doesn't even book and, equally, it's not unusual for him to book and be a no-show. He's only one person, so I can always find a table for him. That's what it's like. We aren't bound to each other and we never ask who else we're seeing. I think of us like Sartre and de Beauvoir, but without the philosophy.'

'It may be that you were one of the last people to see him, Madame. That's why it's so crucial that you cast your mind back and try and fix the date.'

'I have this recollection that he wasn't his normal self the last time I saw him. Usually he would try and charm the waitress staff, but there was none of that. I asked him if he was OK. He said he was, and that seemed to lift his spirits and he revived, so much so that we sat out here way past closing time before going upstairs. It *must* have been the thirteenth. I feel it was fairly recent ... *but* ... it could have been before that, I suppose. Sorry, I just can't be more specific.'

'Well, thank you for your honesty, Madame, and thanks for the tea and the delicious little doughnuts.'

'I think I've wasted your time, Commandant, but I hope I've tempted you to return one day for a meal at Le Saigon. Max will turn up unharmed, I'm sure of it. His type always does.'

They wished each other good night and Ruppert returned home, more than ever thankful that he had a settled life and a wife to go home to.

7.

Over coffee the following morning, Madame Ruppert asked him what the plan was for the day.

'Interviews and more interviews.'

'Who with?'

'It's not so much who with, but in what order. That needs careful planning. I think I'll go first thing to see that architect you mentioned last night. I'll stroll around there now. I'm sure he'll have started early.'

At 8.45 am, Ruppert was inside the offices of Loisel Architecte and been introduced to Emmanuel Loisel.

'Sorry to catch you so early, Monsieur.'

'This isn't early for me, Commandant. I'm usually here at 5.30 am to catch up on paperwork before going on site. You're lucky you find me here at all at this time, a rare office day for me.'

'I understand that you worked on a house in Figuières Folles for Sam Rodgers and then subsequently for Clive

Collins. Is that right?'

'Yes, quite correct. Rodgers did major works to the building, which was originally two very old structures, a farmhouse and an adjoining outbuilding that were divided up into flats. There was a lot of work involved and a lot of money issues, trying to get it done on budget and in the way we both wanted to do it.'

'Did you have problems with the planning department?'

'When don't I have problems with the planning department? That lot are the bane of my life. And you can't argue with them, because you know they have the final say.'

'And Christian Taval? How about any dealings with him?'

'Taval? I thought you wanted to know about Collins?'

'Humour me, Monsieur. I'm trying to get as much background as I can. Who knows how it might help? So . . . Christian Taval?'

'Well, he cropped up when I was working with Rodgers. Very pernickety guy. In the end, I sent Rodgers to see him. I told him that sometimes, if the planners could only meet a real-life client, they can be persuaded to take a different line.'

'Do you mean bribed to change their minds?'

'I didn't say that, Monsieur, *you* did. I've never done anything like that. My professional life would be finished, so I just wouldn't do it.'

'Did Rodgers do it?'

'I never asked and he never said, so I don't know.'

'Did the visit work?'

'Yes and no. Some work was allowed and some wasn't. For example, the proposed swimming pool was refused, but by then Rodgers didn't care about it anyway. He told me that Taval had seen sense on some things and that he himself had compromised by withdrawing the pool application, which he was happy to do because, as he said himself, he'd virtually run out of money by then. A little later, when the work to the house had finished, he decided to sell up . . . with no pool.'

'And that's when Collins appeared on the scene?'

'Correct. And, surprise, surprise, the first thing he did was get in touch with me and ask about putting a pool in. I dusted off the original plans and realised that the planners' refusal had been based not only on objections from the neighbours but also on the fact there was an old disused well exactly where we had originally sited the pool. So, I just moved the location to a different part of the garden and presented the revised plans to Collins. We then got bogged down in the planning procedure all over again. Finally, after what seemed like an eternity, with endless battles with the neighbours and assurances about limiting the hours of use, we suddenly got approval – only last year in fact – and off we went.'

'Did Collins bribe Christian Taval?'

'Again, I don't know and I didn't ask. He didn't tell

me anything other than he'd given some money to the neighbours, the Sims I think they're called. I asked him how he'd persuaded them to withdraw their complaint and he said he'd just gone round and said to them, "How much money do you want to withdraw your objection?" He told me they'd asked for five thousand euros and he paid them that without arguing. He explained to me that when people claim they're acting on principle, it always boils down to money and "How much?" usually solved the problem.'

'What about Madame du Perry?'

'He gave up on her, but by then he was told that he'd got his permission as the Sims were the main issue as they lived next door. Anyway, he got his pool.'

'Yes, I know. I've seen it. Very attractive. But why do you think the planning authority finally gave permission?'

'You mean, Christian Taval again? It's a puzzle, but, like I said, I didn't ask and what's more, I certainly didn't ask why Collins was so keen we used Georges Taval as the main contractor for the the build.'

'You mean, you suspect a deal?'

'No, I mean that I simply didn't ask why Collins had chosen Taval. We put it out to tender in the usual way. Three different contractors as we normally do, and Georges Taval was the middle quote. That's the usual favourite position with house owners. In fairness, he's put in a lot of pools. And yes, Christian Taval's department have given the permissions for those in this area, but then his brother works in other districts too. There's no reason to suspect anything underhand, necessarily, and I certainly was not party to anything. I always impartially put forward the candidates of any competitive tender for the work and run through all their good and bad points with the clients, but I always leave the final decision to them. They're the ones paying the bills, so they get to make the choice. If it goes horribly wrong, us architects can shrug it off as their fault. That's how it was with Collins and Taval.'

'One last question, Monsieur Loisel. When did you last see Collins?'

'I may have seen him in one of the bars around town. I think I saw him at Le Divin – the little wine bar opposite – a while back and we had a brief chat, but I previously saw him properly at the tail end of the summer last year when we finished the pool. He wasn't happy about the mosaics, but he'd designed them, not me. Then he rang me over the winter about a leak, but I said he'd have to take it up with Taval.'

'So you haven't seen him recently?'

'No, I'm sorry. I haven't.'

'Well, thanks for your time, Monsieur. If you think of anything that might be important, please get in touch.'

Ruppert was soon on his way and Bonnet was waiting for him at the Collins house when he reached it.

* * *

As they were both walking into the garden and over to the front door of the house, Ruppert paused, holding the keys.

'There's a strong smell of drains here today. Madame Ruppert first pointed it out the other day.'

'A lot of houses are the same, sir. I'll walk around the house and flush all the loos. That usually does the trick.'

'Good idea, Bonnet. Let's see if that works. I'll make us a coffee. I keep forgetting to bring some milk with me, so, unfortunately, it will have to be black.'

'Two sugars for me, sir.'

Inside the house, Ruppert decided to call Gérard's mobile.

'Good morning, Gérard. Commandant Ruppert here. Look, I'm sorry to bother you at work, but is there any chance you could meet me at the house this morning?'

'I'm not at work today. They've given me a week off because they're filming a documentary about Van Gogh's time at the hospital, and the crew wanted us all out of the way. They've taken over the place.'

'It would be great if you could come straight over then.'

'What's it about? I don't think I know anything else that can help you.'

'I just want to check a few dates with you, Gérard, before I can write up my report for the magistrate. That's all. Nothing to worry about.'

'Very well, I can be there in about ten minutes.'

Ruppert took the coffees outside and Bonnet joined him.

'It's quite a big place, sir; deceptive. It's got six bedrooms and three bathrooms. You wouldn't think it from the outside. I'd be very happy living here.'

'I *bet* you would – happier than Monsieur Max, I dare say. Shame that's not the test for who gets to buy houses like this.'

They sat at the table under the wisteria.

'We've got Gérard coming in a moment.'

'Him again, sir? What do you need to ask him? He's not been much use so far.'

'I think I want to be a bit tougher this time. I can ask him about this smell for a start and a few other things that are troubling me. By the way, I've just had an interesting conversation with the architect who worked on this place with Rodgers *and* with Collins. Even before that meeting, I'd decided to go hard on a few things with Gérard. I've told him I just want to check a few dates. I wanted to lull him into a false sense of security.'

'Sounds like you've got a theory, boss. Do you want to share it?'

It was too late for that because, just at that moment, Gérard came tearing into the garden on his racing bike, dressed as if he was in training for the Tour de France.

He leant his bike against the chestnut tree, took his

helmet and gloves off and walked over.

'Hello, Gérard,' said Ruppert, 'good of you to come at such short notice.'

'You caught me before I was off to Les Baux,' said Gérard, and, noticing the officers looking at his mamil outfit, added, 'to improve my hill climbing.'

'You certainly look the part. Have a seat. Coffee?'

'No thanks.'

Taking a seat and looking first at Ruppert and then Bonnet, Gérard said, 'I hope you don't mind, but I'm due to meet the other members of my club at the car park opposite Glanum in half an hour, so I haven't got much time.'

'This won't take long, Gérard. Don't worry.'

Bonnet was looking puzzled – so was the guardian – but Ruppert, acting as if he had all the time in the world, took a few sips of his coffee before starting.

'Gérard . . . I'd like you to think very carefully before answering the question I'm about to put to you. It's a simple one so a straightforward reply is all that's required. I want to ask you this – do you know anything at all about this case that you haven't told us and want to get off your chest?'

'I don't know what you mean? Like what? What do you need to know?'

'Let me put it another way – have you told us everything you know about what happened to Monsieur Collins?'

'I've given you all the information you've asked for,

haven't I? If there's anything else you need to know, please ask. You know I'll do my best to tell you.'

'Where is Monsieur Collins?'

'You can't think that I know the answer to that question any more than you do, Commandant. He's missing. Where he is, I don't know.'

'The trouble is, Monsieur Paquet, I think you very much do know.'

'Look, I don't know what you think, but I've been as helpful as I can be to all the police I've seen.'

'Have you? You see, I don't think you have. The Tavals and Rodgers have also been helpful and, it's fair to say, the Lieutenant and I have had some interesting conversations with them and with others. But as to the whereabouts of Monsieur Collins, nobody seems to have a clue.'

'I don't know what *they've* all been saying to you. All I know is that Monsieur Max went missing about three to four weeks ago and I was the one who raised the alarm and reported it. I don't know what else to say.'

Ruppert paused, sipped his coffee and took a deep breath.

'There's a well, isn't there? Here in the garden. Tell me about the well, please, Monsieur Paquet.'

At this question, with its injection of formality, both Bonnet and Ruppert saw Gérard suddenly tense in his seat and visibly blanch.

'It's over there . . . by the olive tree, isn't it?' Ruppert asked, pointing to where, at ground level, a large, old, round, millstone sat shaded by the branches of the olive tree.

Trying to speak slowly and calmly, Gérard replied.

'It's an old well, ancient . . . and I don't think it's been used for years and years.'

'I'd like to open it up.'

'I don't think it can be. It's sealed.'

'With that old millstone? I think we can get it off.'

'It's very heavy. I think you'd need heavy lifting equipment for that.'

'It's very heavy, is it? Interesting . . . I don't think that will worry us. There are three of us and Bonnet here used to play rugby for Saint Rémois and had a trial for Toulon once, so I think we can manage it.'

'Can I come back later and help? I've a lot going on this morning with the practice ride and I've got some important errands to run before lunch.'

Gérard had stood at this point and made to head towards his bike. He backed away from the table.

'Stay where you are, Gérard. You're not going anywhere for the time being.'

'I need to make some urgent calls . . .'

'Bonnet will put you in handcuffs if you don't sit down.'

As Gérard sat down again, Bonnet walked around the table and stood behind his chair.

'Why don't you want me to open the well?'

'I don't see the need.'

'Actually, Bonnet, cuff him to the chair with his hands

130

behind his back.'

'Commandant,' pleaded Gérard. 'What are you doing? This is outrageous.'

Once the handcuffs were on and Gérard was uncomfortably fixed in place – grimacing in some pain and discomfort – Ruppert and Bonnet walked over to the well.

'Actually, *this* is where the smell is coming from, sir. Are you thinking what I'm thinking?'

'Do you reckon you can move that stone, Bonnet?'

'I'll have a go. It'll be like clearing out a ruck.'

With some heaving and grunting, like the prop forward he used to be, and with a little help from Ruppert, the old stone was shifted so that it was half off the top of the well. The stench intensified. The top of it had been partially sealed with building plastic, and Bonnet, putting on gloves, gingerly knelt down to draw it to one side. Again, ripe bursts of a powerful and pungent smell hit them and they both instinctively held their noses.

There, slightly curled up in the bottom of the well, no more than six feet down, was the decaying body, still recognisable, of the missing Monsieur Max with his computer resting on his chest as if it had been tossed in like a bunch of flowers into a grave.

'Well, well, well,' said Bonnet.

'I can explain,' shouted Gérard.

'Bonnet, ring forensics and get them round here straight away.'

Bonnet replaced the plastic and went indoors, saying

he needed to wash his hands and get some water. Ruppert thought the sight they had just seen must have rattled him as much as it had himself and he went back to the table and gulped some coffee. Gérard was sitting with his head bowed.

'I think you'd better tell us what you really, really know about all this, don't you?' Ruppert said.

'It was a terrible accident. I didn't kill him.'

'Tell me the story, Gérard, and take your time. You and I aren't going anywhere.'

'It was all about money. Monsieur Max owed cash to Rodgers from the time he'd bought the house from him and he also owed the Taval brothers for work on the pool and for backhanders promised to get the planning permission. They were all pressing him for payment, but he told them the stock market wasn't in the right place and they'd have to wait. The Monsieur had explained it all to me and said it was getting difficult because Rodgers and the Tavals had made it clear that they didn't trust him to pay up.'

'Where's all this heading, Gérard?'

'By this time, early last month, both the Tavals had seen Rodgers and they'd all agreed to confront Max. That was fixed for the evening of the fourteenth. Max knew that's why they wanted to see him and that they'd all ganged up on him, but he still felt he could handle them, because, basically, he thought they were stupid. The meeting was fixed. That's when it went horribly wrong.'

'Why were you involved?'

'Max had asked me to come to the house that Sunday evening because he wanted me to witness the meeting.'

'OK, what happened?'

'They all got very angry. The Tavals and Rodgers were saying he was a dishonourable man and had broken his word. Monsieur Max was calling them all crooks who should be locked up. I tried to keep them calm, telling them to try and work out a compromise, but Max started saying he was fed up with everything. He told them he'd paid fifteen thousand in cash to Rodgers – which I could tell came as a surprise to the Tavals – and he said that was all he was going to pay to settle the bribes. They could bugger off and sort it out amongst themselves. Georges Taval was angry about his money and shoved Rodgers who then had to be restrained by Christian. Monsieur Max was laughing and goading them saying, "You see, Gérard, there's no honour amongst thieves. They're fighting each other now." Georges was incensed and kept shouting, "What about me?" Max then said, "Look, you bastards, I'm going to go to the police in the morning." That was it. Georges just hit him in the face and the Monsieur fell backwards and went down like a sack of potatoes. We checked him and he was dead. I wanted to call the police, but the others wouldn't have it. They threatened me.'

'How did Collins end up in the well?'

'That was Rodgers' idea. The Tavals wanted to put him in the Rhône, but Rodgers convinced them otherwise.

133

He knew about the well from the old plans and so we manhandled him into it. Taval was supposed to have come back by now to concrete it in, but all he managed was to return on a few occasions to put some plastic sheeting under the stone to try and seal the well up.'

'Bonnet, get the Tavals and Rodgers picked up and taken to the station and get a car to come and put Monsieur Paquet under arrest and taken into custody as well. We can do the interviews this afternoon.'

*   *   *

With forensics working in the garden, Ruppert and Bonnet sat in the study.

'What made you think of the well? That was inspired, sir.'

'I wouldn't admit this at home, Bonnet, but it was really Madame Ruppert going on about the watery deaths in that book Rodgers wrote and then, when she came here, she was moaning about the smell. When I met the architect this morning and he mentioned an old well, I could hardly believe it. Everything suddenly clicked into place.'

'Do you think what Gérard has told us is the full story? What do you think the others will say?'

'Have you ever seen the film *Rashomon*, Bonnet? It's basically all about human narrators being unreliable and that facts can be distorted. In the film, a murder is retold by four witnesses in four different ways. That'll be the problem we'll face this afternoon. Our job will be to try and find the truth. I'd like you to be there with me at the interviews, Bonnet, and, by the way, I'm going to recommend you for a transfer. How would you like to work alongside me? There's a nasty murder in Uzès they want me to take a look at.'

'Really, sir? What can I say? Yes, is the answer to your question. I'd like to work with you very much indeed. I think we make a good team. We beat them in the end, didn't we? They lost. We won. That's how I see it.'

'Winning, Bonnet, is a personal journey. It's not about individual victories or indeed anything at all, other than being able, at the end, to look back and say to yourself that you've been as honest as you could have been, and behaved as decently as possible to others. That wasn't the case for the missing Monsieur Max.'

Also from Thorogood

www.thorogoodpublishing.co.uk

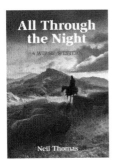

All Through the Night

ISBN paperback: 9781854188960
ISBN eBook: 9781854188977

Written in the style of an old-fashioned Western, this tale of Welsh drovers taking a large herd of cattle from North Wales to London in the 1790s, stakes a claim for these engaging characters to be considered the first 'cowboys'.

Running through this 'Welsh Western', which is rich in adventures and incidents, the storyline has the strong cultural, emotional and human elements that make Westerns so appealing in exploring how people act in the drama of their own lives.

Keeping the Lid On

ISBN paperback: 9781854188984
ISBN eBook: 9781854188991

Set in a private school a little in the past – at a time of turbulence following the death of the Old Headmaster – a sinister thread runs through the attempts to take the School forward. In whose best interests are the figures in authority acting; their own or those in their care?

Spy Without a Cause

ISBN paperback: 9781854189127
ISBN eBook: 9781854189134

With a background of corruption and tax avoidance, this intricate novel is set against events in the early 1980s in Britain's Hong Kong, the Manila of Marcos and Lee Kuan Yew's Singapore.

A young publisher is confronted with personal greed, kleptocracy, espionage and murder as matters move, Eric Ambler style, out of his control.

Available at Amazon and all good retailers.

Printed in Great Britain
by Amazon